PRAISE FOR SHEILA KOHLER

"There is a territory—fictional and psychological—that Sheila Kohler has now marked as her own."

—J. M. Coetzee, Nobel Prize–winning author

"Kohler's work is both spare and sensuous—understated and fraught with tension . . . involving the reader intensely in the narrative."

—Joyce Carol Oates

"Her stories are elegant, smooth, and gorgeously sensual, belying the tension that crackles beneath. Long after I've finished reading one of her stories, the image continues to pulse."

—Amy Tan

PENGUIN BOOKS

Open Secrets

Sheila Kohler was born in Johannesburg, South Africa. She is the author of fourteen works of fiction, including the novels *Dreaming for Freud*, *Becoming Jane Eyre*, and *Cracks*, which was nominated for the IMPAC Dublin Literary Award and made into a film starring Eva Green. Her work has been featured in the *New York Times* and *O, the Oprah Magazine* and included in *The Best American Short Stories*. She has twice won an O. Henry Prize, as well as an Open Fiction Award, a Willa Cather Prize, and a Smart Family Foundation Prize. She teaches at Princeton University and lives in New York City.

OPEN SECRETS

SHEILA KOHLER

PENGUIN BOOKS

PENGUIN BOOKS
An imprint of Penguin Random House LLC
penguinrandomhouse.com

LIBRARY OF CONGRESS CATALOGING-IN-PUBLICATION DATA
Title: Open secrets / Sheila Kohler.
Description: New York : Penguin, 2020. |
Identifiers: LCCN 2019034427 (print) | LCCN 2019034428 (ebook) |
ISBN 9780143135180 (paperback) | ISBN 9780525506850 (ebook)
Subjects: LCSH: Domestic fiction. | GSAFD: Suspense fiction.
Classification: LCC PR9369.3.K64 O64 2020 (print) |
LCC PR9369.3.K64 (ebook) | DDC 823/.914—dc23
LC record available at https://lccn.loc.gov/2019034427
LC ebook record available at https://lccn.loc.gov/2019034428

Printed in the United States of America
1   3   5   7   9   10   8   6   4   2

Book design by Daniel Lagin

For Kathryn Court,
with admiration and gratitude

OPEN SECRETS

PROLOGUE

When she thinks of Michel, it is the sound of his voice that comes to her mind, the musical way he says her name, drawing out the s sound at the end, as if it were a note he is reluctant to let go. She would recognize his voice anywhere, she is certain. After he has gone, she plays the recording of his voice mail over and over again just to hear the sound, his voice coming to her softly, gently, with a reproach caught somewhere in the web of his words. "What have you done to us?" she hears him say.

PART I

BEAULIEU-SUR-MER

June

I

ALICE

1

She is sitting at her desk before the French windows reading, when he thrusts the door open and stumbles through the doorway.

"Goodness," he says, totters across the room, and throws himself down on the small blue love seat in the corner. He is saying something about his client, the rich Russian who has recently opened an account with him at the bank. He had insisted he have a drink with him.

"I didn't know you were coming home for lunch," she says, closing the yellow folder.

"I told Djamilla," he says, referring to the Algerian house-keeper.

Alice has been in the garden gathering flowers. She has placed them in a silver trough on her desk. They are the color of the yellow folder she has before her. She hardly listens to what he is saying. Early afternoons when the sun is this bright are the hardest times for her to concentrate and particularly to practice her violin. These are the moments when her mind wanders to the past.

"It went on forever. He told me the whole story of his life! Didn't spare me a detail. The communal apartment, no bathtub, no hot water. The rats, the kids in the courtyard, the sticks. Made me sit there and drink his vile vodka, which he says is priceless. I'm quite drunk." He interrupts himself to say, looking at her, "But you look very pretty this afternoon, darling."

She has moved her old desk in order to have the view of the sea and the sky, but when she lifts her gaze now, the light is too bright, the water glinting brilliantly this afternoon.

She turns her head, gives her husband a sleepy, grateful smile. She looks at him with the kind of anxious uncompromising love that she has felt since she first met him in Paris so many years ago.

"Your hair looks almost red in this light," he says, staring at her, then leaning his head back, closing his bloodshot eyes, his legs stretched out before him in his gray trousers. He always wears his trousers too short, she thinks. Perhaps he will fall asleep, she hopes, but he stirs and opens his eyes.

"More like white—so many white hairs," she says, putting her hands to her head, though in reality she is proud of her thick dark curls. She feels young and lucky, so lucky to have this view before her, to live in this old villa that Michel bought for them so generously, ten years ago, with its beds of lavender and jasmine, the blue plumbago outside the dining room, the syringa tree in the circular driveway with its delicate branches and pale pink flowers, the yellow laburnum hanging over the iron gate that opens onto the road, the shiny frogs that hide at the edges of the pool.

She feels lucky to still be so slim at forty-two, to be able to play her violin every day, to perform frequently, to have a husband who loves her. She watches as Michel gets up to come over to her.

"No! No!" she says, alarmed, lifting up an arm, leaning forward to ward him off as she watches him sway. "You'll fall. Watch out! Stay where you are." She leans on the yellow folder on her desk.

"I won't. I'm not that drunk, though I've been drinking with that man for hours. I never thought I would escape! I didn't know I had such a hard head for alcohol—better than his!" He knocks his fist against his blond head and stumbles forward, coming toward her. "I don't know how much longer this can go on. He keeps wanting to give me more money! Heaven knows where it comes from."

"Dirty money?" she asks.

"Lots of gold," he says.

"Do people give you gold to keep?"

"Sometimes. Gold can be a good investment, but it fluctuates, of course, like everything else."

"And he has gold?" she asks, imagining the Russian with a briefcase filled with gold bars.

"'Don't you want my money?' he says and laughs. It's become a joke. I've tried to point out the risks, for his sake, but he says he likes my optimism. 'I trust you—we are friends,' he says."

"I see," Alice says uneasily.

"I don't even feel like a real banker anymore."

"You look like a fine banker to me, quite fine," she says sharply. But she is not thinking about him now. He smiles blankly at her. She sighs and asks, "Are things really that bad, Michel, at the bank?" asking, he must surely be aware, for reassurance, which he gives her.

He sways a little as he says, "Not worse, I suppose, than in many other banks. Not much to be done in any case." He looks at her.

"And the Russian?" she asks.

"Oh, he's not any worse than so many others. But I don't want any more of his money. He scares me."

"Why?" she asks.

"Doesn't take no for an answer. We may have to cut back. Make some choices. When I think of what we spent just a few years ago . . ." He stands close beside her now, looking out the French windows, fortunately lifting one hand and leaning on her shoulder, staring at the sea.

"Don't think about it," she says. Then despite herself she asks, "What exactly is happening at the bank? I mean I read the newspapers, but how serious is it for you, for us?"

"I don't really know, to tell you the truth. It's all become too complicated for me," he admits, and changes the subject. "Look at it—the sea," he says, and there is a glint of longing in his pale blue eyes.

He looks older, she thinks, looking up at him, noticing the lines on his thin neck, though he has remained as seductive as always, even now, half-drunk, because of something boyish, youthful, and innocent about the smooth, creamy skin, the narrow waist and hips, the way he stands casually on one foot, like a bird—a flamingo, perhaps—leaning on her. Though he is not tall, not much taller than she is, and his shoulders are not broad, his body is slim, his blue eyes still lustrous, his teeth small and even and almost transparent. He has the sort of physical vulnerability that appeals to both men and women. She has seen men staring with longing at him.

She hopes he is not going to tell her anything too disturbing about his work, this client who is probably a crook, about their finances, the leaks in the floors of the old house. She does not want to hear about too many bad things at once. She feels too cowardly, too frightened. She cannot bear it. She stares up at him.

If she were a painter like her sister, Lizzie, she thinks, she would paint him now, looking at him as he stands there unsteadily staring out the window. She would call the painting *Lost Illusions*.

"In what way will we have to cut back?" she asks despite herself.

"The house. We may have to sell the house."

"Not the house. I love the house," she says. She loves the breadth of the view, the vast blue sky, the sea. She can see a boat in the distance, a white sailboat on the sea, the sails unfurled, leaning so that it almost seems to touch the water with the mast.

He says, "It's the house or Pamela's boarding school."

"Oh! She would be devastated. It's the first school where she has finally—at fourteen!—been really happy. She adores her Swiss school, her friends, that English teacher—what's her name?" Alice says.

"We could probably get a good price for the house," he says.

"I could do more concerts. Perhaps even sign up with an

orchestra. I could get maybe thirty or forty thousand dollars a year. They might even have me in Nice. I could ask Dominique."

"Dominique? Who's he?" he asks suspiciously.

"You remember the conductor?" He looks vague. He never does remember the people she introduces him to, or rarely. "The house doesn't cost us that much," she says a little desperately, though she knows it does, indeed, need repair. She looks around her big room with its pale blue sofa and old gold chairs—such pretty chairs, which belonged to her mother—where she practically lives, where she plays her violin for hours.

"Alice, we can't afford it," he says, and puts his hand on her head, stroking her hair, but she pushes it away, hearing footsteps.

The housekeeper, Djamilla, who brought Michel up, who came with the family from Algeria years ago, is scratching on the open door to warn them of her presence. She announces lunch in her old-fashioned, formal way.

"Monsieur est servi," she says grandly, standing in the doorway in her long black dress, her black head scarf, like some sort of portent of disaster, Alice thinks. She knows the woman would do anything for Michel. Alice laughs and says, "And what about madame?" and winks at Michel, but Djamilla has already left the room.

"She adores you," Alice says, sighing.

"I'm not so sure at this point. Seems rather surly these days," Michel responds. He leans across and picks up the bowl of flowers.

"What are you doing? You'll spill!" she says.

"For the table, such a pretty yellow." But he is spilling water on the folder on the desk.

"Look what you are doing!" she exclaims as he puts the bowl

down and picks up the wet folder, the letter fluttering slowly to the floor. "Come on, let's have lunch. Djamilla is waiting. Leave it—I'll throw it away!" she says urgently. But he is looking at her, has her firmly by the hand to stop her from picking it up. He bends down and picks up the letter. He is holding the thin paper in trembling hands, looking at the writing, the signature. Everything seems to be happening fast. She feels herself growing old in an instant.

If Djamilla had told me he was coming back for lunch; if I had come back to the house half an hour earlier; if I had put the folder away; if I had burned the letter; if it had never been written! Who writes letters today!

He is turning slightly green, particularly around the nose. He is breathing rapidly.

She, too, has difficulty breathing. She thinks of the saints being buried under stones.

"A letter from Luigi?" he says, staring at her pathetically, as though there were some way she could deny it.

"An old one; I had forgotten it was even there," she says sadly. Why did she not tear it up, throw it away? But he has it in his trembling hands and is reading. *I won't be able to save him now.*

Her pity is fast dissolving into a kind of impatience. She wishes he would pick something up, smash something, shout— anything but the sorrow in his eyes. His voice is soft, almost pleading. He blinks.

She remembers how he came up to her that time after the concert she had given in the Salle Pleyel in Paris, how he said in a breathless voice, his blue eyes shining, "You were wonderful!" with such admiration. It was irresistible.

Now he reads aloud, "'Here is no word tender enough for your name.' I have heard that before," he says bitterly, his mouth, once such a tender bud of a mouth, hard and thin, brittle. Suddenly she feels she is looking at someone else.

"Did you answer the letter?" he asks.

"No, of course not," she says, feeling her eyes fill with tears.

"Why not?"

"Because I had nothing to say. It was over, over, over!" She wants to weep. She can hear the clock on the mantelpiece ticking in time to the thump of her heart.

"Oh, Michel," she says, "we will get over it, won't we?" He just stares at her. She is listening to the sound of the wind.

For some reason she thinks of her mother's death. Alice was twelve years old when she found her mother one morning early on the old brown sofa in the house in Amagansett. She was lying there still and gray and alone. Alice knew immediately she was dead, though no one had ever mentioned the possibility that she might die and she had never seen a dead person before.

She had not run to call her father, who was out in the garden, but upstairs into the bedroom where she and Lizzie slept. She told her little sister, only five years old, that their mother was dead. "Mommy is dead," she announced flatly, almost accusingly. Lizzie was in front of the standing mirror and holding her blond plaits with the blue bows. She was staring at Alice in the mirror. Alice will always remember the look in Lizzie's light eyes. "You don't have to cry," Alice said.

II

ICHEL

1

When Alice closes the door on their bedroom that night, Michel goes to his study, throws his book on his desk, gathers up his papers, and paces up and down. He is suddenly full of energy, though it is late, after ten o'clock. He is imagining all the terrible secret words Alice must have whispered to Luigi, the same secret words she has used with him. He needs to move. He holds himself erect, clenching his jaw, grinding his teeth. He finds himself reciting certain passages from Luigi's letter; better to be angry than miserable, he tells himself. *How little we know about ourselves*, he thinks. Where can he go? he wonders. What can he do? He cannot stay here.

He picks up the telephone, calls the Russian at his villa, and asks if they can meet. He says he needs to talk to someone. For some reason he thinks the Russian will understand, and indeed the man immediately invites him, tells him to come to his house.

Michel lights a cigarette and then leaves it in the ashtray to burn before he leaves.

Fire and fury, he thinks as he drives in the dark, taking the long way, the sea route to the villa in Nice. He opens the windows, letting the warm night air into the car. The movement makes him feel better. *If I can just keep moving, moving.*

In the state he is in, it is wiser to leave, he considers. He imagines Alice with a pillow over her beautiful face. He glances at himself in the car mirror and smooths down his hair, which is curling in the damp air.

He has been to the Russian's house before, though never at night. He remembers walking out of the shadows of the study on the second floor, standing blinking on the balcony in the bright light, looking down at the group of men sitting around the table on the lower-floor terrace by the pool and seeing a pink hydrangea in a pot in the middle of the table and the glint of a gun. Could he have imagined such a thing?

As he drives under the olive trees that line the entrance to the grand villa, their silver leaves lit up by lights at their bases, he wonders if this is wise. What is he doing here? Why is he driving to the house of a stranger? What does the Russian mean to him? he wonders. Somehow in his state of raw fury he feels an affinity with the man, who, he is almost certain, has connections to the Russian Mafia. He thinks of him saying, "It's hard to say how much Russian money comes from organized crime and how much came from what was the KGB."

When Michel pressed him to read the fine print on a contract he wanted him to sign, the Russian waved him away. "But you need to know what our fees are, how much we will be charging you," Michel protested.

"I don't need a contract. I trust you. You're my friend. We will make money together," he said, and gave him a hug.

When he rings the doorbell it is the Russian himself who welcomes him, throwing an arm around his shoulders.

"Come on in. What a nice surprise!" he says warmly. He seems genuinely pleased to see Michel. Perhaps he is lonely—a lonely man? So rich and not ugly, but lonely. Michel imagines the Russian's lonely life with all the secrets he cannot share. He has mentioned a wife, perhaps several wives, even a child—what was the name: Sasha or Sergei? Michel doesn't remember—but none of them seem to be around, part of his daily life.

The Russian is in khaki shorts and not wearing any shoes, and his blond hair is disheveled, Michel notices. He wonders if he is already drunk as they walk side by side through the ornate hall, with its gold candelabra, the mauve orchid, and the black-and-white marble floor, down the arched silent corridor and through the glass doors, which open with a sigh onto the pool. The Russian waves Michel into a white painted chair. They sit facing each other in silence, their shadows glimmering in the water of the pool lit up by moonlight. The warm air is scented with honeysuckle and jasmine that grows in big pots at the four corners of the pool. It is very quiet.

The house seems deserted—no one else here, no servants.

"What was it you wanted to talk about?" the Russian asks, but Michel just shakes his head. What is there to say? So it is the Russian who speaks.

2

Michel sees a deck of cards and a bottle of vodka on the table. "Are you a gambler?" he asks.

"Aren't we all? Or anyway all Russians?" he says with a grin, and offers Michel some vodka. Michel knocks back several shots, his temples burning.

The Russian, for some reason, talks of his studies. He has a thick accent but speaks fluent English in a rather low, guttural voice, using his hands as he speaks. He says he was lucky in high school, as he was able to concentrate on a few subjects in which he did well, or he would never have gotten into university.

"Was it difficult?" Michel asks.

"Competition was fierce. There were a hundred places open but only ten for high school graduates, and I was no good at things like chemistry or math, though I had a terrific German teacher," he says.

"So you concentrated on the humanities like I did?" Michel asks.

"Best preparation for life," the Russian says. "Teaches you how to read people, doesn't it? I read lots of books as a boy, books about sport, spies: *The Sword and the Shield*—stuff like that. Later I studied law, because I wanted to be a spy, and they told me at the KGB I needed a law degree."

Michel looks at his smooth face, the narrow blue eyes, the plump, sensuous lips. *Of course you did.* Heaven knows what the man might have done as a spy, whom he might have had assassinated or killed himself.

The Russian looks at Michel and says, "In some ways we are similar, you and me."

"Similar? In what ways?" Michel asks, smiling at him, surprised.

"All those secrets—banking secrets in your case." He smiles, turning his head slightly. "You, too, are good at keeping secrets, aren't you?"

Michel nods and asks himself, in the end, how different is a spy from a Swiss banker?

"When I came back from Dresden—when the Soviet Union was no more—I was lost. What had I accomplished? What was all that work for? All those studies? All the hours I had listened and learned? All the informants I had found. You must feel something like that now with all the names in the papers."

Michel looks at him and nods.

The Russian continues, "I had worked so hard. It wasn't easy." He was poor, he tells Michel, and the stipend they were allowed at the university did not cover his expenses.

"So how did you live?" Michel asks, thinking of the generous amounts his parents had scraped together to send him, the only boy, to Stanford, because they wanted him to have the advantage of an American education, and how his sisters had complained, how their jealousy had been sparked. It was the beginning of his estrangement from the family, he thinks, that and his father's terrible death. Also, they had never really liked Alice. He remembers, bitterly, hearing his eldest sister, Suzanne, saying, "She has shifty eyes"—his brilliant, beautiful American bride! Shifty eyes! He was terribly offended, but now he wonders if Suzanne was right.

Sometimes he worked in construction, which paid well, the Russian says. "Hard, but you could get a thousand rubles for six weeks' work."

Once, when they had some cash, he and his friends managed to buy seats on the deck of a big, beautiful ocean liner going to Odessa. They were made to wait on the quay while the passengers with first-class tickets got on board. Then they got worried they would never get on the ship, so they simply told the attendant they had the big tickets. They had just made it on board when the attendants lifted the gangplank, leaving the crowd of passengers who had paid money for their deck tickets on the quay. "Story of my life," he says with a grin.

He says they found some lifeboats and climbed up into them and used them as hammocks. For two nights he lay there looking up at the stars.

"It was beautiful. I'd never seen something so beautiful," he says, smiling and looking at Michel.

"Best place to be," Michel says, adding, "We should go sailing together, one day."

The Russian nods and says, "I would like that very much. Wait, I have something for you." He grins at Michel and gets up. He goes into the house, and comes back with something in his hand.

"For good luck. It will keep you safe," he says, reaching out to give it to Michel.

Michel looks at the painted wooden object.

"*Matryoshka*, you know, those Russian dolls that fit into one another?"

The Russian screws off the top one, and Michel nods his head.

"Gogol, Lermontov, Pushkin, Dostoevsky, and Tolstoy," the Russian says, and laughs.

Michel puts them into his pocket. "Thank you," he says, wondering if this man could be a friend, a real friend.

Then he tells the Russian about Alice, what she has done to him. "I was so sure of her, so certain she loved me completely, uniquely," he says.

The Russian nods. "I know what you mean." Then he looks into the dark corners of his garden and says, "Do you want me to help?" with a half grin, picking up the pack of cards and flipping them back and forth through his long, lean fingers.

"What do you mean?" Michel asks. "How could you?"

"Well, I could find someone who would take care of the problem for a price." He fans the pack out on the table before him, picking out the king of hearts, the ace of spades.

Michel looks at the cards and at him and for a moment imagines Alice erased like a word on a page: gone her sweet smile, the birthmark on the shoulder, the dark flower between the lithe legs that Luigi, too, has apparently appreciated.

"Nothing life-threatening—just a little lesson she wouldn't forget."

Michel shakes his head. "That's not what I had in mind," he says, and grins. "But thanks."

As he leaves the house and walks to his car, he feels a breath of dark damp sea air wafting up from the shore. All he can hear is the soft sound of the sea and the blood beating in his ears.

III

$\mathscr{P}$AMELA

1

This summer when she comes home from boarding school, there are no trips, fewer clients, and, Pamela understands, there is less money. Her good-tempered father sometimes looks solemn, worried, and cross. "Don't go into finance when you are big; go into science," he advises her. "Be a doctor or an engineer."

They even have a serious argument one evening, the first time Pamela has ever seen her father so angry. They are in his study at the back of the house, and she is sitting on the small striped sofa reading a book for school: *Hard Times* by Dickens. She is reading about Mr. Gradgrind when her father looks up and starts talking about Pamela's school. He is sitting at his desk looking at his little blue agenda, turning the pages. "Getting too expensive for me. What about trying the local school in Nice next term? It's supposed to be quite good. You'd be closer to me and your mother, and it would cost nothing," her father proposes.

"But I love it at Rougemont. All my friends are there. I love my teachers. You went there yourself. You always said you learned so much. I want to do the international baccalaureate, which is much more interesting," Pamela says, surprised her father would even suggest such a thing.

He looks at her as if she has betrayed him. Her calm, orderly, polite father suddenly picks up an old beautiful jug on his desk and throws it at the wall, to Pamela's complete amazement; she watches the pieces shatter like her illusions.

He is irritable with poor Djamilla at times, too, and particularly with Pamela's mother. He complains bitterly about the Americans and says they are all such hypocrites, that they take everyone else's illegal money, keep it in Delaware or Nevada, but do not want their money going anywhere else: "It is not democracy but hypocrisy." He says that the Americans are forcing them to voice out loud what they have kept secret for so long out of loyalty to their clients. People's lives are being ruined by publication in the papers; names are being divulged to the different governments and the papers. It is, according to her father, to everyone's detriment and particularly dangerous to his own.

She has promised her father that whatever happens to her or to him she will always be his brave, good girl. He has impressed on her the necessity for silence about certain matters, what he calls *our secrets*. It is better not to mention any names, any places, and certainly not any conversations she might have overheard. There were certain papers, lists of figures, and secret lists of names of accounts and numbers that were carefully destroyed by burning and flushing down the toilet before leaving hotel rooms.

PART II

BEAULIEU-SUR-MER

August

I

ICHEL

1

When the Russian calls that evening, he tells Michel he wants to withdraw his money. "I gave you my money to make a profit, not to lose it! I want what I gave you back."

Michel says he need not worry. "All under control," he says, just a slight dip in gold prices but nothing serious, nothing to be concerned about, which is what he sincerely believes, or anyway what the investment people at the bank, the quants, tell him. He says the economy is basically sound, that all that is necessary is a little patience, not adding, obviously, that he does not understand every single algorithm the bank uses.

The Russian says, in quite a different tone of voice, that he is not a patient man.

Michel has never heard him speak in this tone, though he has always been aware that underneath the self-deprecating jokes, the intimacy, the charm, there is a sort of rushing underground stream of violence that risks bubbling to the surface under some slight pretext or another. He thinks of the Russian telling him that he was a thug as a boy, that he would jump on anyone who attacked him or anyone else unfairly. "I was consistently rash, physically violent. Often I could barely contain my temper," he has told Michel frankly. Obviously this is not the sort of man one argues with, not the kind who can accept a refusal or a rational explanation of the fluctuations of the market, a need for patience.

Michel suggests instead that they go sailing, as they planned. On the boat they can discuss things calmly. "It's supposed to be a fine day tomorrow. Bring your suit. We'll sail and take a dip." He adds something about this not being the best time to withdraw money. "Sometimes it's best to wait these things out," he says.

The Russian says there is nothing to discuss. It is simple. He wants what he gave Michel back. It seems that all mention of friendship, of trust has suddenly disappeared. The man's voice is angry, rough, rude. He talks to Michel as if he were a stranger— worse than a stranger, an enemy.

"I see," Michel says. He suggests they meet in any case, at the dock in Beaulieu, in the morning, to go for a sail.

"Will you have my money?" the Russian asks.

"Your money is safe, of course."

"All of it?" the Russian asks in a voice Michel has never heard him use before.

"We'll make a plan," Michel replies, though he has no plan, only vague thoughts of ending things, one way or another, of leaving the Russian on the quay and drifting out to sea, or letting him kill him.

He thinks of the morning he opened the bathroom door and saw his father hanging there from the ceiling, his necktie around his neck.

II

PAMELA

1

She wakes when the door opens. With her eyes still half-shut she becomes vaguely aware her father is sitting close beside her on the bed, stroking her hair back from her forehead. For a while she pretends to be asleep, but he remains there patiently. She's aware of his familiar calming smell.

When he bends down and kisses her on her cheek and whispers, "Good-bye, darling," she opens her eyes and looks up at him. She notices his white sailing clothes. She asks, "Can I come?"

Since she learned to swim at four or five, her father has let her steer the boat, trim the sails, tie the ropes with the complicated knots he has taught her, and even hook onto a buoy or throw down the anchor, when she became strong enough to lift it.

If she ever makes a mistake with a maneuver, he never shouts at her, the way she has heard other men do at their wives or children. He always seems delighted with her ability. Unlike her mother, Pamela loves the feeling of freedom and also the precision of sailing, the small space where everything has its place, a contained area to share with her father.

Often, when she is home for the holidays (or in the years before she went to boarding school), her father takes her sailing with him, sometimes for as long as a week. She has her own small cabin with her own shelf, where she puts her books, her cell phone, her computer, and her old toys, covered with a net so they will not fall down. They have even gone as far as Italy, skirting the coast, stopping in many different ports along the way. She likes Ventimiglia, where she can eat spaghetti and talk to the friendly Italian people her father knows there.

Now he responds, "Not today, darling."

"Why not?" she asks.

"A client," he explains.

"I won't bother you."

Her father has taken her along to meet clients. They have met people in grand houses or in fancy hotels, people who were always kind and smiled at her and offered her sweets or delicious dishes and spoke in low voices. Sometimes they left her with their children or a maid for a while.

Sometimes she helped her father pick the gooseberries he grows in their garden. She would take the berries in a little straw basket to some client who was always delighted when her father would say Pamela had picked the berries especially for him or her. She sees herself lifting up the straw basket lined with a bright napkin and smiling, and the lady looking down at her with tenderness.

Once, her father took her with him to London, and they stayed in a fancy club with grand reception rooms and a dining room where everyone whispered at breakfast, though their own room was small and on a high floor and had no key. They had a magnificent tea at Brown's Hotel, and then her father disappeared for a while with a client, going into a private room, while Pamela sat in the paneled lounge on a velvet settee with all the cakes and sandwiches in tiers, reading a book he had left her, while smiling waiters wafted around her. She must have been eleven or twelve, but he still dressed her in a smocked dress with her hair plaited and tied with two big bows, as though she were younger.

"I know you wouldn't, sweetheart, but it's not possible today," he says now.

When she asks where he is going he says, "Depends on the wind."

She imagines being on the boat, the wind whipping the sails. When she turned twelve or thirteen, her father told her that when he traveled business class on certain airlines, he was entitled to a free extra seat, which it would be a pity to waste. He invited her to come along with him and sit beside him and keep him company; otherwise, he said, he would miss her the whole time he was away. When her mother objected that she would be in the way, Michel replied that, on the contrary, she was good for business and put his clients at ease.

She wonders afterward, when he is gone, what would have happened if she had repeated her request to go with him. What if she had insisted? He rarely refuses her repeated requests; her mother is the disciplinarian.

When she asks him who the client is, he puts his finger to his lips and smiles a strange, mysterious smile, the one she thinks of as his James Bond smile. She wonders if it is the Russian she has met with him recently, the one with the sloe eyes.

All the clients she has met are extremely polite to her when she is with her father, particularly if there are packets slipped over a table or a desk, exchanged so fast and so surreptitiously that she sometimes does not notice anything except her father's expression when he has given or received an envelope.

"What's in there?" she once asked when she was quite little, before she realized this was not something that anyone mentioned.

"A little secret! Our secret," he said, wonderfully, mysteriously. "James Bond," he would sometimes say, or "Double-oh seven," in his playful way, raising his blond eyebrows and suggestively opening his blue eyes wide at her.

"And who am I then?" she would want to know.

"James Bond's essential private assistant," he would say.

Now he kisses her again and tells her he loves her, will always love her. He waves from the door. She listens to the familiar squeak of his rubber-soled boating shoes as he walks down the corridor.

She tries to go back to sleep but cannot. Why has he not let her go with him? she wonders. What is different about this outing? She is curious and at the same time anxious. She thinks of all these voyages she has been on with her father. They seem a mysterious adventure, a secret world, something that she understands she must keep between her and her father. She tells her mother and her school friends as little of what happens as possible, so that it seems almost as if it has not happened at all or happened only in a dream. She understands that her presence on these trips is useful to her father's business, though she is not always quite sure what his business is.

When Pamela was five or six she asked her father why he had clients in so many different places. He explained with a smile that he traveled to visit them a lot because the bank was trying to make things easier for them.

"Why? Do they find things to be difficult?" Pamela inquired.

He gathered her into his arms on his lap and said in a low voice, "You see, my darling, the world is such an uncertain place. Things can happen so suddenly and so unexpectedly: revolution, war, change of government. Think of my father, who was so wealthy in Algeria. They had everything—land, factories, vineyards—until the War of Independence, and then they had nothing. He tried to remake his life in France by growing apples in Normandy, but it didn't work out. Never got over it. It really killed him."

Pamela has heard the story of how immensely rich her grandfather had been until the war in Algeria. She understood that the indigenous people, the Arabs, rose up against the French colonizers and took away the land from the French, who were called *pieds noirs*, people who had been there for a long time and thought of the place as their home, but who nevertheless had to leave. She imagined them literally with black feet, though her father's were not black at all but very white and well cared for, with his clipped nails and soft, clean soles. Though he had been a small boy when this happened, three or four, back in the early sixties, he had never forgotten leaving the vast property, all the cars being driven down the driveway, the servants coming to say good-bye, his two big German shepherd dogs given away to them.

He went on explaining things, perhaps then, or at some later date. The sequence of things that happened before or later is sometimes muddled in her mind. She remembers how he said, "Our work at the bank all began during World War Two actually, when we helped certain Jewish families who needed to hide their money. They were able to use a secret number and a made-up name for the account rather than their real name, so that no one knew where their money was except the one banker involved in the transaction. It became very important to keep those secrets. People's lives were at stake. Never betray a secret, darling—that is the most important thing to learn in banking and in life. Never lie or cheat. Honesty and silence, as if a friend told you a secret and you promised not to tell anyone. You would never do so, would you? Do you understand now?" She said yes, though it was all very vague in her mind.

Now unable to sleep, uneasy, and curious about her father's destination, she gets up and pads barefoot in her white pajamas with the blue piping, going through the silent, sleeping house. She goes into her father's quiet study, at the back of the house, with its shuttered windows and the mimosa tree outside. She opens the middle drawer of his ornate desk and slips her fingers to the back to find the secret drawer—he has shown her once— where he keeps some gold coins in a little velvet box and his blue agenda with all his necessary information. "My Bible," she remembers him saying.

She turns the pages to today, August 23. There she reads a

name and next to it a number that she knows must be the name and number of the client's secret account. She presumes her father is meeting a client on the boat to chat about his investments. She considers writing down the information but instead looks at it again and memorizes the name—which is vaguely familiar from her Russian history class—and the number and puts the book back into the secret drawer, where he always keeps it.

III

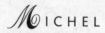ICHEL

1

They meet at the dock at nine. The Russian is waiting for him at the entrance to the marina. Michel leads him directly to the boat. "There she is," he says, indicating it and smiling. Somehow just seeing the smooth shape of the white boat reassures him, makes him think, for a moment, all will be well. The sun is already strong, though there is hardly any wind. The Russian stands looking at the boat, admiring it. "Beautiful," he says. "A Swan?"

Michel nods his head. "Forty-five feet," he says proudly, not mentioning that the boat belongs to the bank. He jumps on board and reaches out a hand to the Russian. "Let's go," he says. The sooner they get under way the better. He doesn't want the Russian asking him to produce his millions in cash immediately.

The Russian, who wears a white cap pulled down low over his forehead and fancy sunglasses, climbs aboard easily and helps with the unfastening of the ropes. An agile man, he seems to know what he is doing, laughing and pushing off, then jumping easily down the steps into the cabin to find a glass of wine, as though he owns the boat, as it leaves the shore.

There is no wind, the sea slick and calm, the heat rising—a brilliant, still, late-August morning. Michel is obliged to start the motor.

The Russian is smiling, sipping as he watches Michel closely. He compliments him on his skill with the handling of the motor, the boat. He is all charm today—in an expansive mood. He expects, obviously, in his arrogance, that Michel is bringing him the original amount of his ill-gotten gains. Michel understands it must be difficult for this man to imagine anyone would not do what he wants them to do. Basically he can only understand two responses to his demands: "Yes, sir," and "No, sir," the latter of which will get you killed immediately, Michel is aware, as he pilots the boat away from the shore.

Despite everything, there is the familiar thrill of moving fast over the water, watching the shore slowly disappear, the expanse of sea and sky and sun opening up before them. Freedom!

The Russian lies out flat on his back, his cap over his face. He seems to be asleep. After a while as the wind lifts, Michel shuts off the motor and hoists the jib, and they progress rapidly across the sea he knows so well. Somehow Michel feels safer the farther they are from the shore, from other people, from civilization. It always seems a miracle to him that the wild wind can be harnessed by a sail and a tiller and directed to carry him wherever he wishes to go.

Eventually the Russian sits up and suggests they take a dip. "Why not," Michel says. He loosens the sails, throws down the anchor in the clear turquoise sea, puts down the ladder. The wind is picking up, the surface of the water choppy.

Michel lets the Russian change first in the small cabin, not wanting the intimacy in close quarters. As he changes he looks at the Russian's heavy gold watch, his thick wallet, his cell phone on the shiny table. Then they stand, side by side on the deck, in their bathing suits, gazing down at the water. Michel glances at the Russian's strong legs, his smooth, hairless chest, not much broader than his own. He realizes that in some kind of tussle or fight they would be evenly matched. The wind begins to blow hard suddenly, the way it does sometimes here.

"Is this wise?" the Russian asks, glancing at Michel.

Michel is not worried. This is his domain, the place where he is most at home. Besides, what has he got to lose? "No problems," he says, and smiles.

The Russian says something Michel cannot quite catch, something ironic, nasty, about his expert skill as a sailor compared to that as a banker. Then he says, "Now I understand how the Swiss banks work. No names on any of the transactions, which means you take a profit when there is a profit, but if things go down it is the client that pays! That's not going to work with me, I'm afraid!" Michel considers a response in kind—saying something about his reluctance to deal with Russian gangsters—but what purpose would it serve? The wind is beating the loose sails against the mast, the waves breaking against the boat.

Moments from Michel's life come to him as he stands there on the deck in the sun in his bathing suit. Like a wave engulfing him, drowning him, he sees the bright beach in Algiers, the pink wildflowers growing in the blond sand, his hand clinging hard to Djamilla's as she lifts her arm to shield her eyes from the sun, the shadow of the wide sleeve of her haik covering him; birds twitter in the ivy, a muslin curtain blows out a window as a classmate leans out and calls to him, "Michel! Wait for me!" but he bicycles on, late for class, his books strapped onto the back, his calves aching as he madly pedals up the hill; a narrow gray street winds before him in the fine mist as he trudges on, the photocopy of the same lectures given year after year clutched in his arms; the sun shines on his desk on a small bowl of blue hyacinths and the photo in its silver frame, Alice with Pamela on her knee, in the quiet, orderly office where he sits, leaning back in his chair before a client in a gray three-piece suit who is smiling with satisfaction at him; Alice is standing on the stage at the Salle Pleyel, so slim and straight in her long black gown, her fine face shining, her head thrown back playing the violin; his darling Pamela, his dearest heart, in her smocked dress, is climbing up onto his knees and putting her little arms tightly around his neck. All these joys, all this effort, all this life has melted away, he thinks; all is transformed from bright ambition, love, and longing into a dull, dark, desperate stream, a gray hopelessness, a cloud of smoldering hypocrisy, lies, deceit of many kinds, into ashes. *What is it all for?* he asks himself. *What is it ever for?*

They will all be better off without him, he thinks. He hears the waves break against the hull of the boat, the wind in the loose jib, the rattle of the ropes against the mast.

PART III

BEAULIEU-SUR-MER

August

I

ALICE

1

For days she does not lock the front door. She does not turn out the lights. She does not go to bed. She wanders through the indifferent rooms of the old house, sure she will hear his voice in the hallway, that he will come home. She cannot imagine he is not coming back.

When the call comes, at twilight, the shrill ringing shattering the silence of the empty house, she hesitates to answer. She stands in the hall by the old black telephone, unable to pick up the receiver, as if it were a volcano about to erupt. Since Michel's disappearance everything feels ominous, as though the threat of death lingers in the air. She can smell it.

All the way to the morgue in the taxi, she thinks he cannot possibly be dead, that it must be a terrible mistake. She is certain of it.

The man at the morgue, a small, dark man with a patch over one eye, forestalls her with a hand on her arm, in the long, silent corridor with its smell of formaldehyde. He stammers in confusion, "I'm so sorry we have to ask you to do this, madame. I know it will be upsetting." He warns her the body was in the water for at least four days and that, therefore, the face might be unrecognizable; still, nothing prepares her for the sight.

When she enters the room and sees the wrapped body lying there on the steel table, the ravaged face tilted up toward her, she is seized with terror and a sort of fury. All her tenderness for Michel evaporates, replaced by horror at the sight of the unfamiliar face, the terrible pallor, the strange hostile expression, almost a snarl.

She screams, "No! No!" though the pathologist is showing her the heavy gold watch he always wore, the one that belonged to his father, with its inscription; the contents of the pockets of his white linen sailing trousers, the old trousers he loved and that she herself often repaired for him; his sodden leather wallet, with a few euros—he never carried much money on him; his driver's license, his identity card, the old shoes he always wore for sailing, with the rubber soles. Then, before she faints in the doctor's arms, she thinks that she hates this body, that it has nothing to do with her living Michel, nothing!

2

When she finally brings herself to tell her daughter what has happened, Pamela responds in an angry voice, "It's not true!" as though Alice were making it up just to break her heart.

"I'm afraid it is true," she says.

Alice dresses carefully for the funeral, as if her dress could protect her: a dark brown designer dress, something soft in chiffon, a little dark veil over her hair. She wears her mother's gold earrings, which hang in two long loops from her ears. She can still feel Michel's fingers touching her head. "Poor darling!" Was that what he said when she complained about having to sell the house?

The church comes to her in a blur of heat and light. Everything seems incongruous, unreal, crowds of people moving as if in slow motion, the white walls too bright, the flowers gaudy, the music too loud. Yet she chose the flowers and the music herself, found the violinists, a young woman and a man who had studied with her at the conservatory in Nice. The minister asked her what Michel's favorite hymns were. Michel had never attended church with her, though he must have gone as a boy. Sometimes he would accompany her to the door on Sundays or come and pick her up at the end of evensong with his habitual gallantry. "You can't possibly walk home on your own in the dark!"

Evensong is her favorite service, with the boys in their white robes singing all the responses in the choir. In a way, she thinks, church has been her connection with her childhood, her English mother: the same prayers, the same hymns she heard in the Episcopal church in East Hampton.

She wanted to tell the vicar Michel had not believed in God. Instead she said he had preferred Mozart.

"Quite," the vicar at St. Michael's, a tall, thin, dusty Englishman who smelled of tobacco, said, and chose the hymns himself.

Alice looks ahead, trying not to see the people on either side. She hurries down the long gaping aisle, clutching Pamela tightly

to her. On one side of the church, she cannot help noticing a
group of elegantly dressed people, strangers, in pale grays and
black, who turn to stare at her and Pamela. Clients, she imagines
they must have been.

Pamela scowls all through the service. She kneels beside her
mother in her pleated skirt and patent-leather shoes, closing her
eyes on the black coffin with its shiny screws.

Mother and daughter huddle side by side alone in the front
row, like an island, with the sea of relatives surging resentfully
behind them. A sort of suspicious silence hangs over all. The
whole family has descended on her from various parts of France.
The sisters, all four of them, whom she has seen rarely during
her marriage and who were certainly not at her wedding, are all
here, en masse. It seems obvious to Alice what they—particularly
the oldest one, Suzanne, the plump one, with her dark thick
hair and big pearl earrings—are thinking. They cast her quick
angry glances from under heavy brows. Suzanne, who sits in
the pew directly behind them, weeps in little sobs, crying
steadily and at length during the ceremony. She goes on crying,
the noise grating on Alice's nerves. *Make her stop!* she wants to
cry out. She sings loudly to cover the noise, "For those in peril
on the sea," though the hymn seems a particularly unfortunate
choice.

The mother, Adèle, who would sometimes come to stay and
shut herself up in the best guest room with her magazines, now
seems hardly visible behind her mask of powder, her dark eyes
blank. She sits stiffly in the pew beside her daughters, her hands
folded in black leather gloves, in her black hat and veil. Alice lifts
the veil to kiss her as they exit the church, her powdery cheek

hot. She smells of peppermints. It seems the mother has disappeared for good; Michel's death has carried her away.

Then there is the moment in the cemetery in the heat, standing under the cedar trees by the grave, the bloodred earth covering the casket. She can feel the perspiration trickling down her arms under her brown dress. Her body is weeping, she thinks. She is afraid of fainting. She reaches for Pamela's hand, but the girl withdraws it from her grasp.

Alice remembers standing beside Lizzie at their mother's grave in the rain and mist. She wishes she asked Lizzie to come back to Beaulieu for the ceremony. She feels surrounded by enemies.

Alice feels the family, even their friends, the whole *pieds noirs* community think she is at fault. She considers they have never liked or accepted her, even after all these years. She imagines they are looking at her and thinking she is too thin, too brainy, too ambitious. "Always too clever for her own good," she has overheard one of them say.

She feels they find her superficial, too worried about her weight, the latest review of a concert, some famous musician who might advance her career. Above all, they think she was too critical of Michel, that she worked too hard, wanted him to work too hard, to succeed at the bank, to make a lot of money, so that she could play her violin.

No one in Michel's family loved music or ever came when Alice gave a concert. They never opened a book. Adèle read nothing but sensational women's magazines. Now Alice is the one who cannot play. Since Michel's disappearance she has not picked up her violin.

At the reception everyone keeps saying that Michel loved sailing best, that he often said that was the way he would like to die. Alice thinks it was Pamela whom he loved best. She looks around for her daughter and sees her standing alone in a corner of the garden under the mimosa tree. She notices one of the unknown guests, a tall thin man with a balding head, wearing a pale linen suit, striding across the lawn with a glass in hand toward Pamela. He puts his hand on her shoulder, leans down to speak to her. To Alice's surprise, Pamela lifts her head, says something to him.

Pamela, who has talked to no one at the reception, refused to eat or drink, is now saying something to this stranger, looking up at him and then suddenly rushing off, leaving the guest standing there munching on one of the hors d'oeuvres, a shrimp, Alice imagines.

Alice wonders what the guest could have said, and what Pamela said back. She goes to find the girl, who is hiding in her room. All Pamela will say, sitting on the bed and drumming her heels against the frilled skirt, is that she wants to go back to school, now! Alice suggests she take a few weeks off to come out with her to visit her aunt Lizzie in America, but she will not hear of it. She insists on going back to her beautiful school near Rolle, the first school where, at fourteen, she has finally been happy. She wants to be with her friends and teachers. There is one whom she adores.

II

PAMELA

1

Pamela rises and stands in front of the mirror on the back of the door of the big armoire in her room. She looks at her pale round face with disapproval. The nose is too wide, she thinks, pinching it between her finger and thumb. The cheekbones are too wide, too. She scrunches them together with one hand, puckering her lips. Her mother always says she has her grandfather's Hungarian lips. She wishes she had her mother's narrow, delicate face, her straight slim nose, her thin lips, her fine dark curls, and above all, her mother's small, slanting, secretive eyes. She never quite knows what color they are or what her mother is thinking. Her father was much easier to read.

Pamela looks at her own eyes in the mirror, and they seem too dark and large, and they show too much. She fears the man in the garden saw clearly that she knew what he was looking for. It came to her suddenly when he asked for it, and her discovery must have shone clearly in her eyes.

She had noticed him first when her mother and she had walked up the long aisle of the Anglican church. Her mother's arm was gripping her fiercely around her waist. For a second her gaze had met the man's, as he turned his head to stare at her. He was standing at the end of a row near the back of the church. She had remembered something about him then, something sunny and pleasant, something that had happened with him when she was much younger, though she did not know what it was. She had been distracted at that moment by the weight of her mother, who was propelling her forward in a sort of desperate dash to get them into the front chairs before the altar, where they could sink onto the cushions on their knees and hide their eyes from the awful sight of her father's shiny black casket with the gold screws. She had sunk down, put her head into her hands, and shut her eyes. She kneeled beside her mother, and tried to pray to her father for help, though she knows he never attended church or believed in God or the afterlife. It is her mother, the believer, who chose the church and the music for the ceremony.

Pamela has difficulty believing her father is dead. She wanted to see his face one last time, but her mother prevented her. She said it would be too upsetting, that her father had been in the water and no longer looked like himself, and that in any case, by the time her mother had brought herself to tell her that he was dead and not just missing, the casket had already been closed.

Surely, though, he must be somewhere near, she thinks, looking up at the cream ceiling with the yellow moldings in her big room with its four-poster bed, armoire with the mirror, and her desk. He cannot be gone completely from her life. She can still hear his voice, the sound of his light laugh. She can still feel his warm hand in hers. She can smell his special, clean smell. He always made her feel calm, protected. Above all she knows he loved her so much. Surely, he could not have left her alone.

She cannot believe that she will not find him inside the thick walls of the quiet bank in Nice where he spent his days. It was a place she found so reassuringly clean, orderly, and safe. There were the green marble counters and the cream leather couches and all the polite people, who moved fast and efficiently and spoke in low voices. Outside the windows bright red geraniums grew in the window boxes in the sunlight, as though, she always thought, all that money must have grown flowers.

When she was very little, she imagined his work as sitting at a desk counting great heaps of money. Soon, though, she realized that what he did had more to do with people than with figures. She understood even when she was quite young that her father was not particularly good with figures. He never carried much cash on him and always counted out carefully the small amounts he did dispense. Yet people always liked and trusted him, which seemed quite natural to her.

Everyone loved her father, Pamela thinks. Everyone spoke easily and with pleasure to him. He never made them feel they had done something wrong but instead encouraged them in whatever they had chosen to do. He had so many friends and acquaintances.

After all the weeping and the innumerable people kissing her cheek, breathing down on her, whispering how sorry they were, how much her father had loved her, how proud he was of her, pressing her hand, she thought she had finally managed to escape and to stand alone in the shade in the garden. Then the man came up to her.

She had noticed him again in the garden at the villa. He was huddled in a group of people on the terrace. They were all dressed smartly in beige or gray, talking in low voices with solemn faces, their heads close. They were drinking white wine and eating hors d'oeuvres that a maid in black with a white apron was passing around on a small silver tray.

Looking around the garden, he had spotted her standing there on her own. He still had a glass of wine in one hand and was munching something, his thin pale lips moving, as she watched warily, with a feeling of unease, as he strode purposefully across the lawn toward her.

There was nowhere to hide, though she had often hidden behind the big lilac bushes or the mimosa trees, playing hide-and-seek as a small child with her father or her mother or Djamilla. Now, however, she could not do so. At fourteen she is tall, after all, already taller than her mother. It would not have been seemly to duck and run. Besides, she was curious. She had the vague feeling she had seen this man before, perhaps on one of her visits with her father.

The man came up to her and put his hand on her shoulder in a friendly yet proprietary way. She stiffened but was obliged by politeness to remain where she was, saying nothing, only looking down at the blond, sandy soil around the tree. He looked down at her and said without smiling, in slightly accented French, "Your father was very proud of you, always talking about how clever you were, what a good memory you have, how many poems you can recite by heart in different languages."

Pamela said nothing, though he paused then and seemed to expect a response, looking at her inquiringly. Perhaps he wanted her to recite a poem. But she wasn't going to do that. There seemed nothing to say. It was all true. She knows her father was proud of her and boasted about her memory and her facility with languages. Her father was good at them, too; he could speak some Italian, German, and even a few words of Russian, a gift she has inherited.

When she was alone with her father he would speak French. In the car, when they went away together on his business trips, he would often tell her about his own father and mother and the luxurious life they had once lived in Algeria on an enormous property, before they'd had to flee to France with almost nothing left. He talked about the beach where he went as a little boy with Djamilla and the bright light and all the flowers.

During these conversations, which she thought of as their private ones, they always spoke French, whereas when her mother was with them, they spoke English, though her mother's French was good, too. Still, Pamela felt French belonged to her father and her. Pamela was born in America; her father had begun his training at an American bank at the start of her parents' marriage. He spoke perfect English without an accent. Still, he seemed different when he spoke French—more natural, more at ease, more himself. In English his voice sounded different, he made different gestures, he walked differently, and he even wore a different smile. He sounded more businesslike, more official, stiffer. She preferred the French father.

Though she indeed has an excellent memory, she could hardly agree with the man without seeming conceited. As he spoke, she recalled his name, Boris Primakov, though she had met him only once, two or three years earlier. It came back to her in a rush, in that moment in the garden, that they had once gone to his big modern house outside Geneva, a grand house on the lake, where she had gone swimming in a new striped bikini her father had bought her. She could see the clear, shining water, and she remembered wading in, the mud between her toes. She remembered that her swimsuit had been blue and that she'd had a white cap to match with a little blue flower on the clasp.

As the man finished off his glass of white wine, he looked at her narrowly, and then around at the other people gathered there. She noticed his nose looked very thin, pointed, and shiny, as he said, "You probably knew your father better than anyone else here," which seemed a strange thing to say, and which Pamela hoped was not true. Now that he is no longer here, she thinks of all the things she does not know about her father, all the things she would have wanted to know, but it is too late.

As the man leaned down and whispered in her ear, she remembered how his wife had called him Bory, a childish nickname that had seemed odd to her, as he was so tall and quite old, with his thinning hair and lines around his thin lips. She could also recall the splendid breakfast they had eaten on the terrace at his house by the lake: heaps of scrambled eggs in a silver tureen and ham with cloves and honey, different kinds of cheese, sweet cakes with cinnamon and nuts, crispy rolls with strawberry jam, coffee in a big shiny pot, and frothy milk. She remembered how her father had said something to Boris at the breakfast table when his wife had left to go inside, and how Boris had replied, glancing at her, "Little pitchers have big ears."

Her father had responded, "But carefully guarded ones. No worries with that one. Closed as a clam."

Now Boris asked her, "By the way, did your father say anything to you before going sailing? Do you happen to know who was going with him or anything about him?"

Pamela shook her head and said quite truthfully that her father had not told her where or who he was going sailing with.

"I have a hunch that if your father had told anyone where he kept his important information, it would have been you, his darling daughter," said Boris, staring at her with his little slit eyes.

Did he know, then, about her father's agenda, his little blue book where he kept the important information about his clients, in its secret drawer? Pamela remembered at the same time the name of the account, a strange foreign one she had been trying to recall all through the funeral, and even the number in the blue agenda. Did Boris see this knowledge in her gaze?

She excused herself as politely as possible, as though she had suddenly thought of something urgent she had to do. She walked fast through the crowd, fixing her gaze on the glass door into the living room, so that no one would come up to her, and then quickly, quickly, she ran up the steps and down the long corridor into the silence of her own room.

Silence seems safer to her now. She is afraid of what she might say, or what she might reveal through her eyes. What did the man make of her abrupt departure? In any case it seems wiser now to hide in her room and prepare for her return to school. She opens the armoire and reaches in to take out her favorite blue jeans and a soft black sweater, to be worn in the evenings, when they are allowed to change out of their uniforms. She rescues her old gray stuffed lamb, which she has hidden at the back of the high closet shelf and has almost forgotten, a remnant from her early childhood, which she puts to her cheek and strokes with one hand, while she sucks her thumb, something she has not done since she was a little girl.

She is afraid Boris now knows that she knows something important. She wishes her father were here to tell her what to say and then to take her with him on his boat across the smooth, clear water, as they did so often before.

Now, she thinks, looking at her shoe rack, trying to decide which shoes to take to school, she will never go on a secret voyage again with her father. It feels quite impossible to imagine. Her life seems suddenly gray and bleak and without hope.

III

ALICE

1

It is Michel's old nanny, the Algerian housekeeper, who convinces Alice to let Pamela go. "Let the pet do what she wants," she says. "Her father always said if anything happened to him, she should go back to boarding school, where she'd be safest." Then Djamilla sets about washing Pamela's clothes, ironing everything, marking each item with her initials, and packing her suitcase, smoothing each article flat. She comes with Alice to the train station in Nice to make sure Pamela gets off without too many tears.

Djamilla is the only one who understands that for the first few weeks after Michel's funeral, Alice is afraid. Djamilla does not leave her side. She brings food on a tray out onto the terrace, as if Alice were ill. She sits beside her in silence as she eats, or just holds her hand. Alice is afraid of the dark, of silence, of noises, of being alone in the big villa, as a child would be. Djamilla even sleeps with her the first night they know Michel is no more, lying beside her chastely in the double bed in the guest bedroom at the back of the house, leaving the bedside lamp lit, not even closing the blinds, and lying heavy and silent beside her like a nun in her long white nightdress.

Alice cannot sleep all night. She listens to every creak and murmur. She thinks she hears a door open, footsteps. She gets up and walks quietly around the empty rooms, turning on lights. She has the terrifying impression someone is in the house, someone who should not be here. She hears footsteps in Michel's study at the back of the house, and when she goes to the room and stands in the doorway, it seems to her she catches glimpses of someone moving around his desk in the shadows. For a moment she is convinced he has come back to her. She even says in a whisper, "Michel?" But when she turns on the light no one is there, but she feels certain the papers on his desk have been moved. The middle drawer is open. Who left the drawer open?

The only reassuring thing is the sound of Djamilla's loud, steady breathing in the bed next to her, where, trembling, she retreats. She huddles under the covers, until she eventually falls asleep in the early morning. When she wakes, Djamilla has slipped silently out of the bed and gone to the good baker down a side street, still in her slippers, to get Alice's favorite breakfast.

"You must keep up your strength for Pamela's sake," she says. She comes in with a tray, bringing a hot croissant with butter and the fig jam she makes from the tree in the garden, and a big cup of café au lait. She opens the curtains with a sharp pull, letting in the brutal, bright light of the summer day, the impossible palm trees, the scintillant sea.

Alice thinks how Djamilla switched allegiances before Michel died. She, who had been so critical of Alice, became understanding and kind. Alice is not sure why, but the woman seems changed, almost as if she knew what was going to happen, or as if Michel got on her nerves, as Alice had before. Or perhaps it was Djamilla who got on his nerves by seeming cross with him, disapproving, and short-tempered.

2

At the inquiry the notaries and the insurance people will all be against her, Alice knows, so she begs Djamilla to come with her. "I can't go on my own," she insists for once. Djamilla looks at her and sighs. For some reason she refuses to go in the taxi with Alice, as though she wants to make this as painful as possible for herself. She shuffles up the steep hill in her head scarf and her habitual black dress, panting in the heat. She says what needs to be said at precisely the right moment.

They sit in the shadows of the shuttered office. "Tell me. Were there perhaps health problems?" the notary, Larieux, asks, looking from Alice to Djamilla.

Djamilla shakes her head and retorts firmly, "Never sick a day in his life! Healthiest man I ever knew."

"Professional problems?" the notary tries again.

From behind his vast empire desk and his tortoiseshell glasses, Larieux stares at Djamilla and then at Alice, but neither of them says anything, though Alice has always thought that

Michel was not cut out to be a banker and had difficulties with numbers from the start. She herself is much better at math, and she can even cope better with the complexities of a computer than he could. He never talked to her much about his work, particularly since he began at the Swiss bank, except when he would occasionally bring people to dinner—hard, silent banker types in pin-striped suits, who never said much despite his valiant efforts to entertain them.

"Problems of the heart?" Larieux insinuates with a slight sneer, looking not at Djamilla now but at Alice, who says nothing.

It is Djamilla who speaks up: "Not as far as I know." After all these years she has not lost her accent. She even maintains Michel did not know how to swim, which is a blatant and perhaps even unnecessary lie.

"Are you certain?" the notary asks. "A boy from Algiers? Such a skilled boatman? I had the privilege of going out with him once on the *Élysée*—such a beautiful boat."

Djamilla talks about the sudden strong wind and the possibility of a fall overboard, as though she knew something about sailing or has prepared for this line of questioning or has been told what to say. She sits bolt upright in the shadows of the shuttered office before the large, imposing desk.

"No one knew him better than I did," Djamilla says severely, which is probably true, a frown like a knife on her otherwise smooth forehead. "I was there at his birth, and I brought him up."

The words that come to Alice are "and at the hour of his death." Where was Djamilla the day Michel disappeared? She, too, seemed suddenly to have vanished. She also wonders if

Djamilla took some of Michel's papers with her. Where is Michel's little blue agenda?

3

For weeks Alice has not slept. She feels something close to chaos. Sometimes there are moments when she almost forgets he is gone, and at others, the memory floods her mind unbearably, like blood rushing to her head. There are moments, too, of indifference, coming from a distance, like that of a woman who has never had a husband.

She shuts up the elegant old villa and sells it fast—too fast, perhaps. She takes the first offer she gets, from the man next door, a Russian oligarch. When the wife visits she asks only, "Tell me frankly, madame, does the roof leak?"

Alice says no, truly, it doesn't. She does not add that it is the floors that weep in the winter. In her state of rage and grief she does not want to imagine the seeping damp of the floors. She even sells some of the silver for a song—the wedding tea set her mother-in-law gave her, a pretty fruit bowl that she misses now—as if to spite herself, or was it to spite Michel? How could he have abandoned her?

Did she spoil everything? She sees his face, his pale blue eyes, the inquiring half smile, the eyebrows raised in disbelief. She hears herself say, "It was nothing—nothing—ashes!" How did he drown? How could he have been swept from his big beautiful boat, the place where he wanted most to be?

She decides to wear the dark chiffon dress she wore for the funeral on the voyage to America. Somehow, she is loath to leave the dress behind as though it has become part of her identity. She is going back home to Lizzie, her little sister, to her mother's old house in the country.

PART IV

AMAGANSETT

September

I

1

Lizzie takes the Cannonball, the fast train that stops in East Hampton. It is a quick trip, even though she must take a bus from there to Amagansett. She walks quickly to the house. She wants to get there before Alice.

There is a fine drizzle coming down, but she strides on in her black jeans and short boots, lifting her face to the wet air, dragging her wheeled suitcase. *When you arrive, don't break my heart, please*, she thinks. She was planning to speed out here with Sergei in his white Jaguar. Now she will never see him, either, again.

She looks for the key in the gray electrical box on the side of the house. For a minute when she lifts the lid she cannot see it, but when she slips her finger inside and feels for it, she is relieved to find it and draw it forth. She remembers once coming here late at night, not finding the key, and having to drive all the way back into the city. "The key to the country house," she finds herself saying aloud, going through the thick pink rhododendrons, which have grown wild, to open the blue front door.

It must be almost a year since she has been back. At their father's death, the sisters gathered in sorrowful silence by his bedside. Then they rented the house out. Now everything has changed, but this place seems the same, she thinks with relief, as the door opens easily. The drizzle stops, and her gaze is drawn up, as it always is, by the sudden bright afternoon light, the blue of the September sky, and the beating leaves of the tall magnolia tree, seen through the circular window. The great height of the living room ceiling lifts her heavy heart. Despite their lack of funds, she is glad that their attempts to sell the old house have failed.

Inside all seems exactly as it was: the faint smell of apples that the cleaning woman must have picked to fill the silver bowl on the mahogany table in the dining room; the upright studio Steinway with its two silver candelabra; the threadbare oriental carpets; and the worn leather sofa, where one or the other or both of them have often slept under the fan in the hot summer nights, talking, laughing, and endlessly weeping.

Lizzie looks up at her big bright paintings of chairs, which line the walls: the green Matisse-like one that presides prominently in the middle of a big painting, the bold blue-and-white-striped one with its severe straight legs and arms, the curved Louis Quinze one that is covered in bright yellow, and the spindly one with the lattice back. Each of them represents a different member of the family, though she has never told Alice which one she is.

Lizzie remembers how Alice, as an aspiring dancer, was

afraid of being too tall but stopped growing when she turned thirteen or fourteen and got her period. Alice turned out to be the shorter, the more delicate, of the two Konrad girls, though she became a musician and not a dancer.

Long-legged Lizzie climbs the stairs fast with her small suitcase and her big leather handbag, a gift from Sergei on her thirtieth birthday. She will not think about Sergei now: *Turn, turn my heart to stone*, she thinks.

She will take the small bedroom and leave the best one for Alice, the one that looks out onto the walled backyard with the pool and the apple trees. She throws her suitcase on the bed. She pulls up the blinds to open a window. She can smell the dead leaves, mixed with something living. She still cannot believe Michel is dead. She waits anxiously for Alice to arrive to find out what could have happened.

The silence in the old house at the twilight hour suddenly saddens her. It feels threatening. She is used to the sounds of traffic, the call of sirens in the busy streets of Brooklyn.

Lizzie left the city as soon as she could. In her distress and confusion she struggled to find what she needed in her untidy studio: her cell phone, under a pillow; the charger, dangling from a wall; her credit card, on the floor. She already feels exhausted after only two weeks of teaching. How will she get through the whole semester? She and Alice are both hard workers, though neither of them has made much money with their work, Lizzie's painting and Alice's music.

She lies down on the brown leather sofa with its yellow occasional cushions, where her mother died. She is almost asleep when she thinks she hears a car in the driveway. She thinks how strange it is that neither of the sisters has a husband. She hears the front door open, and sits up on the sofa as Alice comes into the living room in her brown chiffon dress with her shining face. Alice extends her arms, flexing her fingers in joyous anticipation of the hug, rushing to embrace her.

"Alice!" Lizzie says, her eyes misting, tears running down her hot cheeks.

"Forgive me for being so late. It took forever to get through customs, and then the taxi got lost on the way to the jitney stop. Thought I'd never get here," Alice says, as Lizzie lets her fold her into her arms.

"Look at you!" Lizzie says, leaning her head back, thinking how beautiful her sister is.

Her hair seems damp, clinging to her forehead in restless curls. Gold loops glisten in her little ears. It must have started drizzling again, Lizzie thinks, looking up now and listening to the sound of soft rain falling outside.

Lizzie has a sudden memory of Alice coming into the room and announcing that her mother was dead in a cold, dry voice. She remembers standing in front of the mirror and looking at her braids and her own pale face. She remembers Alice telling her she didn't have to cry, taking her by the hand, leading her down the stairs and outside into the yard, and sitting in the orange plastic boat in the sunshine and holding her, while singing her Brahms's "Lullaby" to put her to sleep, the one their mother used to sing so beautifully to them both.

Alice swings her leather backpack onto the floor as she says, "I wanted to get here before you did." She has lost weight and has dark circles like ash beneath her dark eyes, but they are still what their mother had called hazel. Her dark hair curls softly around her beautiful face.

She was their mother's angel, her best girl, and after their mother died, their father's best help in times of trouble. Everyone said she was so, so good! Their mother would look at her and shake her head in wonderment and say, "Alice was just born good. I didn't have to do or say anything to her. She arrived on day one with a strong, moral soul."

She was the one who carried the sticks back and forth endlessly for Lizzie to build the tree house in the yard. Sometimes Lizzie wondered what it must feel like to be constantly called an angel, and whether Alice has always behaved like one.

Lizzie says, "I'm just so glad to see you. How are you? How is darling Pamela?"

Alice says, "I brought some wine for us to drown our sorrows," and takes the bottle out of her backpack. The two sisters walk into the kitchen together, holding hands like children, Lizzie thinks.

In the kitchen, with its clock over the sink and the hum of the refrigerator, Alice opens the bottle of red wine. Lizzie takes out their mother's best cut glasses, slightly chipped around the rim, and a tarnished silver christening bowl engraved with their mother's name out of the old-fashioned glass-front kitchen cabinets. She fills the bowl with mixed nuts. They go back into the living room and sit side by side on the sofa in front of the empty fireplace.

Lizzie leans toward Alice and asks, "Do you want to talk

about it? It's so awful. I just can't believe it. He was so lively, so much fun. He always made me laugh. I can still see him pretending to be a Parisian taxi driver, jamming on the brakes."

Alice shakes her head, wipes her glasses, and says, "Don't! I can't. Not now. We'll talk later. You tell me how you are. I want to know everything, everything. The painting—how's it going? What are you working on? What's happening with Sergei? Is everything okay?"

Lizzie makes a face and thinks of Sergei's treason. If only she could feel indifferent to all that!

"I'm trying to finish a huge painting—lots of color," she says, grimacing and waving a hand at the splashes of paint on her black jeans and low black boots. "And Pamela, my beautiful niece, my godchild—how is she? She adored Michel."

Alice shakes her head sadly and says, "They were like this," crossing two fingers to show their bond.

An image of Pamela as a small child comes to Lizzie. She sees her in her white embroidered nightgown, her blond hair loose, climbing sleepily onto her father's lap, nuzzling her head into his shoulder.

"Honestly, I don't know how she is. You can try calling. She will sometimes do FaceTime, and maybe she would respond to you, but mostly she doesn't. Says she's too busy with her classes, her homework, the school play, something. She was a convincing Nurse Ratched in the school play. Imagine!"

Lizzie shakes her head. "Impossible," she says.

Alice says, "In a white uniform with her long hair caught up in a bun and a severe smile on her face."

Lizzie looks at Alice, and they both sigh. "I just wish she had come with you, poor sweetheart," Lizzie says. "She must be suffering, and we could all have gone swimming together or running on the beach—I don't know, made a cake or played Scrabble!"

Alice nods and says, "She's so fond of you. Honestly I think she loves you more than me. I so wish she were here with us." Lizzie holds Alice's small hand.

"The beautiful villa?" she asks. "That beautiful view of the sea? Did you at least get what you asked for it?" Lizzie sees the palm trees, the curve of the bay, the blue sea shining before her.

"I got enough. There were just too many memories," Alice says, shuddering and sipping her wine.

"What will you do? Where will you live?" Lizzie asks anxiously, biting a thumbnail.

"I have to decide. Pamela loves her Swiss school."

"That's where one wants to be at fourteen," Lizzie says.

"I'm not sure that's where I wanted to be at fourteen."

Lizzie remembers how she herself talked to her dead mother in her mind constantly. "That was different," she says, sighing. "All we both wanted was Mother. Have some more wine."

Alice shakes her head and says, "I'm going to take you out to dinner. I've got some money of my own for the first time in my life. We can share it. Maybe we can even keep the old house, as Mother wanted us to. I'll pay the expenses."

"You have enough money?" Lizzie asks, frowning.

"That's the only good thing: the sale of the villa and lots of insurance money. Michel had doubled the coverage. I had to fight for it, considering the circumstances."

"He doubled his life insurance coverage, just prior to the

accident?" Lizzie asks, bewildered. "Why did he suddenly do that? He was in midlife and in good health."

Alice says nothing, just glancing around the familiar room, where their mother died so rapidly of lung cancer, straining for breath. She would lie on the old leather sofa she and Lizzie are sitting on now, smiling bravely, and ask for her oxygen.

Then Alice looks at Lizzie and says, "Somehow this is where I've wanted to be since Michel disappeared: back home with you," and she reaches out to clutch her sister's hand hard, looking into her eyes. "You are my family."

Lizzie feels the tears come into her eyes. She wants to weep in her sister's arms, tell her of her trouble, but she holds herself erect, biting her lip. She will not burden her poor sister with her tears. Alice, as the elder girl, has always set her an example. Lizzie tells herself she must be brave, carry on, do the right thing.

Now Alice says to her sister, "Maybe I'll just stay on here and take care of the house for you. I've always loved Mother's house."

"Wouldn't it be wonderful if we could keep it?" Lizzie says. She, too, has always loved the endless sand beach and the rough sea.

Alice says, "Perhaps here I could find peace again. I could buy out your share. Pamela could come for her holidays."

It was their mother who had bought the gray barn-shaped house, with the last of her inheritance, and left it to her two girls, though their father had lived here until his death, making only music and not much money.

Lizzie remembers the place filled with glad sounds, a summer house where the two sisters would come with their friends, boyfriends, acquaintances, everyone running in and out from the round white table under the apple tree, through the dining room into the kitchen, spilling drinks or tea, while carrying the scones they had baked, stepping barefoot through the French doors in their bathing suits, dripping wet from the pool, where cries and splashing and laughter filled the air.

She thinks of Christmas, when the sun-filled rooms resounded with music, their father in the role he loved best: playing Berlioz on the piano in his silk waistcoat, pursing his plump lips in concentration, Alice on her violin; or carols with everyone singing in the corner by the Christmas tree, which they decorated every year with the same wooden ornaments Lizzie had made. Alice had the best voice: "Lift thine eyes, oh! Lift thine eyes to the heavens," she would sing so plangently, lifting her green-gray gaze, the light behind her head like that of a Fra Angelico angel.

Dearest Alice, Lizzie thinks, leaning toward her, her sweet, affectionate older sister, the one who was best at math and music, the one with the most powers of concentration, the constant, determined one who went to Barnard and studied philosophy and graduated with honors. Lizzie looks forward to spending some time with Alice on her own. No one else knows her secrets, her sorrows like Alice.

"Let's go somewhere nice for dinner. I'm suddenly starving, couldn't eat on the plane, and then there was the bus. It must be three in the morning for me. Let's go and eat. We won't go far. Let's go to the Mexican down the street. Is it still open?"

Lizzie nods her head. She finds herself saying, "I was hoping Sergei might drive me out here," not looking at Alice.

"He didn't?" Alice says.

"No, I walked from the bus stop," Lizzie says, putting her

hand to her damp hair, looking into the empty fireplace, her eyes filled with tears.

Alice asks, "Something happened with Sergei? Weren't you supposed to have lunch with him today? Is he still . . . ?" Alice looks at Lizzie and raises her eyebrows suggestively.

The two girls look at each other. "I'll tell you later," Lizzie says, and takes her cell phone from the back pocket of her jeans. "Shall I book a table at the Mexican restaurant? Friday night, you know."

Alice nods her head.

The two girls walk arm in arm down the darkling street, past all the familiar houses with their turrets and steep gables, their smooth lawns, and the neat front yards, the familiar damp smells of the hedged spaces, the grass and the chrysanthemums wet after the rain, but what Lizzie continues to see is Sergei's face, the amazement in his dark eyes as she stood before him with the gun in her hand.

2

They are led to a table for two in the shadows at the back of the crowded restaurant. Lizzie sits with her back to the street, facing Alice. They order margaritas, and Lizzie leans across the table and takes Alice's hand. She asks her, "Can you forgive me for not coming out? Leaving you alone?"

"You mean to the funeral?" Alice asks, taking her light green drink from the waiter, sipping.

Lizzie looks at her sister in the dim light of the restaurant and sees her suddenly as though she is a mysterious, unknown woman. Alice does not look her forty-two years, Lizzie thinks. So slender, with her long neck, her short curls, her mysterious sloe eyes, her gold earrings, which belonged to their mother. Lizzie remembers Alice saying, "You take the earrings. They look best on you," but Lizzie made Alice put them on, looking at herself in the mirror and smiling. Such a beautiful face, Lizzie thinks, though Alice wears no makeup, and her hair already has a few strands of white at the temples.

Lizzie nods, looking at her sister from across the table with concern.

Alice answers immediately, "Oh, no point spending all that money. I didn't expect you to come back. You'd been there in June. So expensive, particularly at the last minute and at the height of the summer."

Lizzie imagines August on the Côte d'Azur: so hot and crowded, the sun blazing down day after day.

"I knew you were working away. Fortunately, I had Djamilla. She was wonderful," Alice says.

Lizzie says, "I thought you disliked that old woman, who was always criticizing everything you did. Every time you cooked something for Michel or even tried to arrange the flowers. Always spying on you. Went through your papers, didn't she?"

"She was jealous and controlling, and I did hate her, but oddly, after Michel died—well, actually, even for a while before he died—she was completely different. At least she didn't look at me as if it was my fault," Alice blurts out.

"Your fault! How could it have been your fault?" Lizzie protests, snapping her breadstick sharply in the air.

"It's obvious that's what they were all thinking," Alice says, looking down at the tablecloth.

"What were they thinking?"

Alice shakes her head as if to clear the thought away. "In some ways it was true. Michel should have been . . . I don't know." She waves her hand in the air, looks at her sister.

"A history professor, perhaps?" Lizzie suggests. "He was so knowledgeable—had read such a lot, knew a lot about French history, French literature, Russian literature, was always talking about Flaubert, Maupassant, Camus, Tolstoy. He could speak so many languages, had such a good ear."

"Everyone kept saying how sailing was what he loved best," Alice says sadly.

"And you! He adored you, too," Lizzie adds.

"They kept insinuating, of course."

"Insinuating what?" Lizzie asks.

"Insurance, doubled coverage, made things much worse. It was as though he had prepared for it. Those notaries, the insurance people were awful—so, so snide with all their questions, and charging a fortune."

Lizzie asks, "But why would he? Such a happy man, he always struck me as so even-tempered, so happy-go-lucky. And so loving. He loved you so much, Alice! He was always talking about you, how clever you were, what a wonderful musician, your legs! And jealous, no? He couldn't let you out of his sight. And he adored Pamela. He was so good to everyone around him, generous to a fault, even to that awful old nanny who was a pain in the neck."

Alice begs her sister to change the subject. "Order something to eat; I'm going to faint. What do you want?" Lizzie has little appetite at the sight of her sister, tears running down her cheeks. "So sorry," Alice apologizes, taking a tissue from her handbag, wiping furiously at her eyes.

The two girls have always kept their feelings to themselves. They were taught to chest their cards, not in words, but by example. Their English mother would sing "Onward Christian Soldiers," laughingly, but she meant it. Or she would say in French, "*Tout est pour le mieux dans le meilleur des mondes*"—All for the best in the best of worlds—quoting from Voltaire's *Candide*, on whom she had done her thesis at the Sorbonne. The sisters have always maintained at least a semblance of harmony and calm.

There has rarely been any open strife or jealousy between them, though they went through one period in their lives when they did not speak to or see each other for months. Lizzie was not really sure why. Their struggles were of another kind. They both struggled valiantly with their art: Lizzie starving herself on black coffee and oatmeal to make money as a model in order to paint, Alice giving innumerable private lessons, coaching untalented children who could not play a note, so that she could play her violin at night. Her rich students were often spoiled, rude, recalcitrant. They came late and unprepared. It was nerve-racking and exhausting and paid badly.

Alice and Lizzie lived in cramped quarters in a studio with a loft they built themselves on the Lower East Side. They ate spaghetti and wore cast-off clothes they bought at thrift shops, until

Alice consented to marry Michel—good-humored, happy-go-lucky Michel, but was he then so happy? Was it all an illusion?

3

Now Alice weeps without restraint. Lizzie leans across the narrow table and kisses her on both cheeks. "Don't cry, please," she says. "You never do!"

Alice, who is so soft and sweet and smells of vetiver, looks into her eyes. "So sorry," she says again, obviously ashamed at her lack of self-control, blowing her nose.

Lizzie asks, "How did it happen? Do you think it was really an accident?"

Alice pulls a cautionary face. "Order another margarita," she says. "Tell me more about you. You look pale. Is everything all right?"

Lizzie looks at her and shakes her head. "I've done something really stupid this time!"

"What do you mean? You look terrible, Lizzie! Have you been up all last night?"

Lizzie realizes her eyes must be bloodshot and puts her hand up to cover them. "I need another drink," she says, lifting her arm. She waves to the waiter with the mustache, who comes rushing up to take the order, standing there in his crisp white uniform, while Lizzie looks at the menu.

"What's happened? Something with Sergei? Did you finally give him the boot? Did you break a plate over his head, like I told you to?" Alice asks.

Lizzie shakes her head again and asks for another margarita.

Alice looks at her and says, "And now my man, my darling Michel, who was so suitable, so adorable, is dead! Dead! Dead!" She laughs uncontrollably, the tears still rolling down her cheeks.

Lizzie finds herself saying, "I tried to put mine in the same state."

"What on earth are you saying?" Alice asks, and when Lizzie just shakes her head, she adds, sniffing and apparently startled out of her own sorrow, "What did you do?"

"I can't believe I did it. I was just so angry! Finally, I got angry. As if someone other than me were there, another person entirely. Someone else acting for me, taking over. I didn't think for a moment. I just did it," Lizzie says, making fists.

"Angry with Sergei? You did something to him?" Alice asks.

Lizzie doesn't answer. Instead, she nods her head. "She was there when I came in the door. He'd invited me for lunch. I was early, as usual, but this time, instead of walking around the block, I just walked up the steps and went in." She sees Sergei's redbrick Federal-style house on Grove Street in the Village with the old stone steps leading up to the front door, and the big chestnut tree.

Alice nods. "Go on."

"I was so excited to see him—hadn't seen him for ages. He'd been on business in Siberia."

Sergei was always traveling to Siberia on business—something about aluminum, he told her. She stares off into the distance, biting a hangnail, her hair falling around her face.

"And so?" Alice prompts.

"He had promised caviar, champagne, and I, like a fool, had bought him flowers from a shop down the street. Such a pretty little bunch of red roses. Imagine—red roses! Running up the steps so eagerly in my best dress with the full skirt, the white one, like an idiot. For lunch! I had a key, of course."

Lizzie remembers waltzing in the front door so gaily, going into the dark hall, with the painting of the gardens on the wall, feeling flushed, pretty, her blond hair loose on her shoulders.

"And so, what happened?" Alice asks.

"There they were. He was holding her in his arms in the hall, kissing her amorously on the mouth, like in a photograph or a movie, with her back bending."

"Who was she?" Alice asks.

"The skinny, small French one in her black beret. I think she once worked with him. Remember the French girl, the one both pretty and ugly at the same time, as the French say, with the thick lips and the red lipstick and the pale cheeks?"

Alice looks blank.

"You know. You must have seen her at parties at his house."

Alice looks at Lizzie vaguely. "Thick lips?"

"Anyway, when I came in, she rushed off, or I thought she'd rushed off. You must have met her. She must be nineteen. How could he?" Lizzie says, thumping her fist on the tablecloth, breathing hard.

"What did you do?" Alice asks.

"I don't even know how to do it. Do you remember when Father taught you, with the bottles on the wall? I refused to practice with you," Lizzie says.

"You would never kill a fly, let alone shoot at a man. You

didn't shoot him, did you, Lizzie?" Alice says, clapping her hands together in her fright. "You couldn't have."

"Let me drink first, and then I'll tell you." But she tells her right away, before the drink arrives. "I did fire at him," she says.

"At Sergei? Did you hit him?" Alice asks.

"Of course not."

"Where did you get the gun, anyway?"

"It was in his desk." Lizzie remembers how he showed it to her once: a Russian revolver that had belonged to his grandfather, that he'd brought from Russia. He'd kept it forever in his desk drawer, he said.

"And you took it out and fired?"

"I wasn't thinking of it beforehand, I promise," Lizzie says, remembering how she walked into the book-lined room as though drawn by a magnet.

"I remember putting down the roses on the desk, opening the drawer, and there it was. It looked like a familiar old dog with a snout."

"Then what happened?" Alice asks.

"He followed me into the room, spouting apologies as usual, telling me how much he loved me, how desperately sorry he was, that I didn't understand, that he was getting an ulcer, and on and on, until I couldn't stand another word."

"So, you took out the gun?"

"I just held it for a moment, and then, somehow, it went off," Lizzie says.

"But you didn't hit him?" Alice asks.

"No, no, I keep telling you I have no idea how to aim. The bullet went clear through the fancy molding of the ceiling."

"Does anyone know? Was the girlfriend still there in the house, for God's sake?"

"She heard the shot from the steps and came running back in."

Lizzie imagines the girl in the beret going down the steps quickly, bracing herself with her hand on the railing, hearing the shot, and running back into the house.

"I just stood there, holding the gun. It was the strangest feeling—though I had missed completely, I sort of felt taller, more commanding, looking at them both over the barrel of the gun. They looked so utterly amazed and, well, aghast, terrified, as if I might shoot again."

Abruptly, Lizzie's cell phone rings. She scrambles to find it, dumping out the contents of her big handbag, spilling lipstick and combs and a wallet across the table, as she grabs it and rises, abandoning her belongings with her sister, walking among the tables, which are filled by now, a Friday night, holding it to her ear as she goes out into the falling rain.

"Well?" Alice asks when Lizzie comes back. "Was it the police?"

"Don't be silly, of course not. No one called the police. It was Sergei, who wants to come out. I just ran off when the girl came in. I thought I'd never see him again."

"Perhaps that would be better," Alice suggests with a sigh, but Lizzie cannot help smiling and blinking. Suddenly the room seems too bright with its garland of colored lights strung up across the ceiling, too filled with glad noises, the laughter of a woman behind her, the sizzle of a fajita.

"You mean Sergei is on his way out here?" Alice asks.

Lizzie smiles and nods.

"He'll have to sleep in the attic," Alice says firmly.

Lizzie pulls a face. "We'll sleep on the sofa, if you like."

Alice tells her to order something expensive, and Lizzie com-plies, ordering a bottle of wine, steak fajitas, and dessert, and tucking in. Alice, too, eats an entire steak fajita, as though this talk of death has made her hungry again.

II

ALICE

1

That night, unable to sleep, Alice puts on her dressing gown and leather slippers and goes down the steep, slippery stairs they have both fallen down as children. She carries a pillow and a soft blanket with her and falls asleep on the old sofa in front of the empty fireplace.

There she dreams that she sees Michel as he was the last time she saw him alive, in the early morning light, when he came to say good-bye. He is wearing the clothes she saw in the morgue: white linen trousers, a transparent shirt, and his blue rubber-soled shoes, which squeak as he walks toward her while she lies sleepily in her bed. With the light behind him he already looks like a ghost, and in the dream, as in life, he is asking her for an aspirin. Where did she put it? He has a headache, he says. She lies propped up on her big pillows reading.

And then in the dream he is standing in the doorway, a slender shadow of a man, waving good-bye. He already seems distant, though she can see he is smiling his sweet, open smile. Then his face becomes blurred, transformed, his expression contorted into a ghastly grimace, the one she saw when she went to identify the body.

When she wakes, shuddering, from the dream, the doorbell is ringing insistently. She decides to ignore it. She is not going to open the door for anyone. Whoever it is can just go away. Her head aches, her bones ache, and her mouth is dry. She drank too much wine, too many margaritas. Her sister drank more than she did. She, too, must need an aspirin. Yet Alice is the only one awake, lying there on the old sofa with the big windows above her that let in the early morning light and the figure of the magnolia tree, shaking in the breeze.

She has always been the lighter sleeper. She turns over on the wide sofa and finds Lizzie, who must have slipped down the stairs, too, and joined her during the night. She is sleeping heavily beside her, lying neatly on her back, her big hands folded over the blue blanket, like a reclining statue. She is perched on the edge of the sofa, her blond hair spread out on its brown leather.

Her darling Lizzie! Mother's pet with her blooming cornflower blue eyes. Her lambchop. A murderer or, anyway, an aspiring one. She wonders if Lizzie could have invented the story, but somehow it sounds all too real. Yet she does not seem to be suffering from remorse. On the contrary, she smiles slightly in her deep sleep. What if she had hit Sergei?

Alice is so glad to have Lizzie lying there beside her, whatever she has done, glad not to be alone. But why doesn't she wake up and answer the damn door? Surely, she can hear the ringing, too, even in her sleep. What is the matter with her? Alice sits up and carefully lifts herself over Lizzie's legs. She pulls on her navy blue silk dressing gown that was lying on the end of the sofa and stumbles into the entrance hall. For a moment she imagines that it is Michel, not dead after all, that there has been a terrible mistake, that the pale body she saw in the morgue was just an illusion.

2

She opens the front door slowly and peers out to find Sergei standing there in the glare. He grins sheepishly, a wide grin, long legs astraddle in his tight dark blue jeans. He is disconcertingly real.

"Alice, so sorry if I woke you," he says.

"We were asleep," she says crossly. She is tempted to close the door in order to preserve her moment of hope, her image of Michel alive and well, coming back to hold her in his arms, but she can see Sergei is not going to melt into the early morning light. He must have caught the first train from the city and walked from the station, as there is no sign of a car in the driveway. "Well, I suppose you'd better come in," she says, leading him directly into the kitchen. She is not going to wake Lizzie yet, but she will offer him some coffee.

"That's very kind of you," he says, whispering dramatically.

"I suppose it's the least I can do, since I just learned my sister fired a gun at you."

He responds with a grin and says disarmingly, "But I deserved it."

Alice glances up at him, at his unshaven cheeks, the dark circles under his eyes, adding, "I suppose you did."

"Fortunately, she's not a very good shot," Sergei laughs. "My grandfather's ancient World War One Beretta. Imagine—a hundred years old and still loaded. I had no idea Lizzie was such a firebrand." His dark hazel eyes glimmer at her. Obviously, the idea appeals to him.

How strange men are, she thinks, and wonders why he would have kept a loaded gun in his desk drawer. What sort of company does he keep?

He looks around the kitchen with its big windows, its glass-front cabinets, its long faux Spanish table. He asks with a grin, "Forgive me, but do you by chance have anything to eat?" He sits down, stretching his long legs under the table, expecting to be served. "I got up so early for the first train out here and didn't even have time for a piece of toast!"

Alice looks at him for a moment, the blond hair falling on his forehead. Here she is once again serving this unfaithful Russian, who has spent so many summers with them in the villa in Beaulieu-sur-Mer. Michel loved him, she recalls. She opens a cupboard.

She remembers the two of them sitting out on the terrace of the villa, talking for hours, Sergei telling stories of his father, a thoracic surgeon, who had been arrested during one of Stalin's purges in the late 1940s on trumped-up charges. Thanks to an influential patient, he had been released after an attempt at suicide by throwing himself down some stone steps. He was brought home on a stretcher with his back broken. But instead of becoming an invalid, he had recovered and gone on with his surgical practice. In 1959 he was allowed to settle with his wife in Moscow, where Sergei was born. Alice remembers Sergei saying that though politics was never mentioned in their home, it was understood that the Soviet regime was evil incarnate.

She finds a round loaf of brown bread and some strawberry jam, which Lizzie must have brought from the city. At the sight of it she, too, is suddenly hungry, probably from jet lag. It must be later than two in the afternoon for her: lunchtime. "Would you like an egg?" she asks, opening up the refrigerator and finding a carton of eggs and a tub of butter.

"Make it two," he says, smiling at her eagerly in his disarming way.

When Sergei has his coffee, several thick pieces of brown toast with butter and jam, and the two eggs, she sits down opposite him and joins in.

He looks at her and smiles, saying, "Alice, you are wonderful. You put together a splendid breakfast in two minutes. Can you forgive me for barging in? Lizzie told me about Michel. So sad!" And, as his hazel eyes fill with tears, he reaches out to take her hand. "I loved Michel. He was always in a good mood. Always had a kind word or a joke. We had such interesting conversations! And he was such a loving father! I can see him in your garden in his old gardening hat and green gloves with all that lavender, the lilac, the red peonies—like Chekhov in his dacha. And he accepted us all with our faults, never judged."

She would like to reply with "Almost," but instead, she adds, "I know he loved Pamela and me." She remembers overhearing someone saying Michel had chosen the less interesting of the two Konrad girls and wonders why he picked her. He had always said it was her good brain and the dark beauty spot on her shoulder. Was that all of it? she wonders now.

"He could not have been over fifty, could he?" Sergei asks.

"Fifty-four this past March," she says, remembering how Michel would stare at her and say her eyes were the color of willow leaves.

"It's impossible. How did it happen?"

Alice says nothing—what can she say? She just shakes her head, but she is moved by Sergei's obvious distress, his genuine sympathy. She thinks again of how strange people are, what a mixture of good and bad, how they continue to surprise her. Michel was very fond of Sergei, she knows and says so.

Sergei says, "It was mutual. He was very good to me—so helpful to me, to my friends." He sips his coffee and looks at Alice. He asks, "What could have happened? A boating accident, as Lizzie said? A sudden strong wind?"

Alice sighs and says, "That's what they told me. They think he must have been knocked overboard. They did an autopsy, and apparently there was a slight blow to the temple. He had been missing for days when they found the body in the water."

"He went out alone in his boat? Did he ever do that?"

"I was surprised, too. I thought he was going with a group of friends or colleagues—that's what he told me, though I don't remember who they were. He left so early in the morning—oh, it's all so confused in my mind now. I didn't pay much attention to what he told me at the time, I admit. He had so many friends, people who liked to sail with him. Clients. Often, he was the only one who really knew how to sail. But he was such a good sailor, and he loved just having people with him on the boat. You know how generous he was."

"I do, I do," Sergei says.

"The boat actually belonged to the bank, I believe. And he did take clients out often. Perhaps this was one of them."

Sergei asks, "So he seldom went out alone?"

"And even if he had, he was such a fine sailor—I was not in the least worried about him. I never really worried about him when he was sailing. He loved it so much. It made him happy." Alice remembers Michel laughing and saying there were two things that made him really happy: sex and sailing.

"Did they ever find the boat?" Sergei asks.

"No, I don't think so—it must have been swept out to sea. On a small beach somewhere nearby they found . . ." Alice looks up and sees Lizzie standing in the doorway in Alice's blue shorts with the white stripe down the side and a clean white shirt, which she must also have found in Alice's suitcase or in a closet. Her blond hair with its reddish highlights is brushed neatly on her shoulders. She stands in the doorway, looking at them and smiling.

Though Lizzie is much taller than Alice, they are similarly slender and have often borrowed each other's clothes. Both sisters have exchanged outfits when necessary—gloves, coats, hats, even shoes, in a pinch, and these shorts and shirt look much better on Lizzie than they do on her, Alice thinks.

Alice has a sudden memory of Lizzie posing for nude photos to make money in nothing but a chiffon scarf on some beach somewhere or in a warehouse. Lizzie was always better endowed than Alice. Breast-feeding her child for six months seems to have consumed her very flesh, Alice thinks.

What long, smooth legs Lizzie has. How young and lovely she looks. What a fresh flush in her cheeks. Surely she deserves a faithful man, Alice thinks, looking at Sergei, who is gazing at Lizzie, his eyes shining, as Alice puts her hand to her own cheek, feeling the dry, flaking skin. Since Michel has disappeared she feels a hundred years old. Loss has done that to her and so has love. Love can be a terrible thing, she thinks. Will this unexpectedly violent reaction of Lizzie's keep Sergei in line from now on? Russians seem so volatile to her—such extremes of emotion.

Lizzie comes and sits down at the kitchen table beside Sergei and sips from his coffee cup. "I see monsieur has been served his full English breakfast," she says, smiling a thank-you at Alice.

He turns to her and says, "Do you want to go for a walk on the beach? Such a lovely day," putting his long arm around her shoulders and kissing her on her smooth, flushed cheek. He looks across the table at Alice, having apparently forgotten Michel for the moment, and says, "A dangerous lady, our Lizzie!" Alice smiles and shakes her head in wonder as she watches Lizzie's cheeks flush a deeper crimson.

Sergei and Lizzie stare at each other for a moment and then get up and walk out together into the living room, Sergei draping one arm around her shoulders. They are almost the same height and walk together easily. Lizzie turns her head on her long, graceful neck. She waves at Alice with a little smile.

"Thanks for making breakfast. Back soon, and we'll bring lunch," she promises.

"I'll be here, waiting for you," Alice says, which turns out not to be the case. Moments later she hears the telephone ringing.

This time, when she picks up the receiver, her hand already trembling with premonitions of disaster, it is the headmaster of Pamela's school in Switzerland, Mr. Burns, who says in his Scottish accent that he regrets to inform her that Pamela disappeared this morning after breakfast.

PART V

ROUGEMONT,
SWITZERLAND

Saturday Morning

I

$\mathcal{P}$AMELA

1

There are some winding stone steps that lead down from the top lawn at Pamela's school into a sunken garden. Some of the steps are broken, and lizards live in the chinks. The small round garden has wild bushes of bamboo, bulrushes, and stunted trees, and in the middle a fishpond with goldfish and pink and white water lilies. Small birds sing in the branches almost fiercely.

It's a quiet shady space where the girls and boys go if they want to speak privately of secret things. There is a wooden bench under a willow tree, and a narrow winding path that leads through the bushes and under the trees to a small iron back gate that opens onto the road. It is here that the man comes up to Pamela, with the sun behind him. He is not a tall man and he wears wraparound dark glasses and his hat pulled down low, shadowing his face, which she cannot see clearly. For a moment she thinks it might be her father. Then when she sees what he has in his hand she feels as if it is a scene in a book or a film, not quite real, something that cannot be happening to her. She thinks of her father saying: *You see, my darling, the world is such an uncertain place. Things can happen so suddenly and so unexpectedly.*

She has been back at school for a few weeks when it happens one warm, sunny Saturday morning around ten o'clock. Things have not been as she expected, not at all. It is not that everyone has not been kind; they've been extremely kind—that is part of the problem. The girls have treated her especially kindly, gingerly, almost as if she were terminally ill or disabled in some serious way.

On her arrival in the dormitory with her suitcases, which Djamilla had packed so neatly, with all her clothes marked with her initials, several of them came up shyly, one by one, and asked if they could help her unpack; they brought her little gifts of chocolate or hand cream or cards of sympathy that they had made especially for her by hand, coloring them with somber colors and writing kind words in old-fashioned script or in their best hand—"I am so sorry for your loss," most of the cards read—but once this was done, obviously, they could not think what to do or say next.

Whenever she entered the dorms or the classroom or approached a group of girls in the garden, expecting the old giggles and snide jokes and familiar snickers, she found instead a sudden and awkward silence. After the first few words of greeting and expressions of sympathy, the girls stared at one another sadly. They smiled at her, bit their bottom lips, twisted their hands, or pulled at their hair. The boys were even worse. They would turn red or pale. They had no idea what to say to a girl whose father had just died, so they said nothing, or just nodded and smiled and moved away, as though she had some sort of disease they might catch.

At first Pamela tried to put them at ease. She would say something cheerful or tell a joke, but the girls looked at her askance, as though she had committed an unforgivable faux pas. *Are you heartless? Didn't you love your father?* their eyes seemed to say. Or if they knew her better, *You don't have to pretend to us that you are not sad; we know you must be.*

In class, too, where Pamela waited eagerly to join in the conversation with an answer to a question, as she usually did, her arm waving in the air, the teachers smiled at her kindly and said they did not expect her to participate for a while. They passed her by. She was welcome among them and could attend classes if she wished, but they would not call on her. She did not have to do any of the tests, in which she always excelled, and she was told that if she missed the readings she could easily make them up later. If she would prefer to skip classes altogether, they understood. It was such a lovely, warm fall, the teachers said, and smiled indulgently.

"Take advantage of our beautiful garden—it has such a soothing effect," the headmaster, Mr. Burns, who came from Scotland and whom they called Haggis, murmured to her after chapel in the morning, holding her hand.

And the last days of September were exceptionally fine. The light was white, the leaves turning gold, the lawns still a vivid green. The world seemed startlingly lovely to her, as though she had never seen it before, as if to show her how precious every

moment was, how fleeting, how nothing lasted, least of all those
we love. Her classes, where she was obliged to be silent, where
some dolt said stupid things she could not contradict, were
dull, so Pamela roamed often in the school's big garden on her
own. She wandered under the trees, feeling lonely and homesick
and wishing she had gone with her mother to visit her aunt. She
missed them.

She thought of them in the big house in Amagansett, where
she had spent so many summers, particularly when she was
small, when her grandfather was alive and before her father had
moved to the Swiss bank, which had sent them to Nice. She
thought of how Aunt Lizzie would have welcomed her and would
have understood how she felt: so sad but, after all, still alive,
ready to eat and laugh and cry. She would have curled up with
her mother and her aunt on the old leather sofa and talked all
night. Maybe she could even have gone swimming in the sea
with Lizzie, who, like Pamela's mother, is such a good, strong
swimmer. She remembered autumns when the water was still
warm and the beaches deserted, and she had ridden on the waves
on her mother's back. How could she have been so stupid? Why
hadn't her mother insisted? Yet when her mother or even her
aunt called or texted she did not respond. She couldn't admit
now she had made such a silly mistake by coming back to school.
She felt ashamed.

She spent most of her time on her own. Even her favorite
teacher, Miss Johnston, the one she has always admired, seemed
to shun her after their tea together. On Pamela's return, the
teacher invited her to her room and offered her tea with milk in
a special green cup with a gold rim. She brought it on a little tray

with a special cake with raisins and rum, which she kept in a tin. It was something she had never done before. Pamela was afraid she might break the precious cup and she didn't really enjoy cake with alcohol in it or even tea with milk, but felt obliged to eat and drink.

Also, the tea and cake were accompanied by a long homily on the afterlife, which embarrassed Pamela. Miss Johnston, a woman with short curly hair who wore button-down shirts, sat opposite her in an armchair, leaning earnestly forward toward Pamela. The teacher kept smiling at her, showing her rather long teeth, which Pamela had never noticed before. She waved her big hands and talked with so much enthusiasm, and in such a desperate effort to convince, that her saliva came flying like so many small projectiles in the air at Pamela, who had never seen her favorite teacher so excited. She talked about "the angels in heaven," saying Pamela's father was now with them, was actually one of them, which annoyed Pamela, and which, with the flying saliva, made her want to giggle inappropriately; she felt like a baby. Who believed in angels at fourteen, she wanted to ask. She could sort of believe in some vague benevolent or even bearded God, but angels were part of a child's world and not an adult's. She felt much too grown-up to believe in angels.

Pamela can still remember making an angel out of papier-mâché at school when she was a very little girl. She could not imagine her father as an angel with white and pink feathery wings and a wide skirt, his head encircled by a gold halo. It seemed ridiculous. It was hard enough to believe he was no longer a presence in her life without trying to imagine him as part of the angelic host. He still came to her constantly in her dreams.

He looked so alive, and would tell her not to be sad, that they would soon be together again on the boat. Sometimes, she was sure she caught a glimpse of him in the street when they were allowed to go up to the shops to buy candy and magazines, or even standing near the big iron gate that led into the driveway to her school. He still seemed to lurk in the shadows of her mind, so present in her life.

With the teacher she tried to bring the conversation back to the subjects they had discussed before her father's death. They'd had such interesting conversations about literature, arguments about the books she loved; they were reading *Jane Eyre* in class, and she wanted to talk about the poor mad wife in the attic, someone she had always felt sorry for, locked up and lonely, or the passages about Jane's understandable boredom, and even the meaning of life. Did it have a meaning if they were all going to die anyway? What was the meaning of her father's brief life, his death on a windy afternoon on the sea in the boat he loved? Why didn't the woman talk about Pamela's living father or his real death rather than angels? But Miss Johnston looked sad and uncomfortable when Pamela tried to talk about her father's life and death, and after a while Pamela got up and went into the garden alone, which was where she was found on the Saturday morning by someone who she thought for one moment might be her father.

PART VI

AMAGANSETT

September
Saturday Morning

I

1

On the almost-deserted beach Sergei kisses Lizzie in the morning light. "Look!" he says, waving one hand at the steel blue sea and the white sky, his face lit up. "Look how beautiful it is!"

It is one of the things Lizzie likes most about Sergei: his ability to take pleasure in the beauty of the world around him. She finds him difficult to understand, calm and contained much of the time but capable of reacting suddenly with explosive anger. But she does know this about him: that he loves the light, the landscape. He has often attended her exhibitions, and those of painters she admires. He has generously bought some of her work and hung it on the walls of his many houses. According to him the greatest artists were first Tolstoy and then Tchaikovsky. He puts Kandinsky third on his list.

"Beautiful," she says, staring at the white sky, the shining water, his face. They have the blond sand and the calm dark sea almost entirely to themselves, so early on a Saturday morning in September. A sole walker with his dog can be seen in the distance. It is still so warm Lizzie is almost tempted to take a swim.

"Want to go swimming? Bet the water is still warm. There's no one here," she proposes suddenly and recklessly, though she has not brought her suit with her.

Sergei stands back, looks at her, and says she has the most beautiful legs in the world.

"Come," he says, but leads her away from the water. He takes her by the hand and they go into the dunes, where they lie down side by side in the white sand. Lizzie lies on her back, her arms behind her head, gazing up at the pale sky.

Sergei turns to her, smooths her hair back from her face, and tells her he loves her so much, truly, will always love her. "It was so awful when you ran out on me before I could explain. I was so afraid I would never see you again," he says, his face crinkled like a child's. He bites his thick lower lip.

She has heard this before. It is what makes it so difficult for her to leave this man. Somehow, he manages to present his infidelity as great suffering for him—for *him*! She feels he does suffer, and she ends up comforting him instead of leaving him.

She knows all of this probably has something to do with his lonely adolescence, his early emigration from Russia at sixteen or seventeen, in the late 1970s, to America. She can imagine him as a tall angular boy, all elbows and knees, wandering the streets, lost in a strange city where people spoke another language, finding himself alone without his parents, who could not obtain exit visas and both died before they could join him. The Soviets refused to let his parents leave in the early 1980s, though they tried repeatedly to obtain visas.

His father, first demoted from his prestigious position as a researcher at the Institute of Poliomyelitis and Viral Encephalitis, then lost his job when Sergei emigrated. The officials had terrible ways of punishing parents for what they considered the sins of their children. His father died shortly after of a heart attack. Sergei has always felt responsible for their hard lives and ultimate penury.

But the memory of standing there, a gun in her hand, comes to Lizzie now. She sits up and hugs her knees, looking out at the implacable steel-colored sea. She sighs and says, "That's what you always say, and I am sure you think it is true, Sergei, but if you really love me so much, how can you make me so unhappy? How could you have had that girl there? I was so excited to see you, rushing up the steps of your house with those red roses like a damned fool!"

Sergei sighs, too, sits up beside her, and takes her hand in his. He lifts it up into the air, pulling at each one of her long fingers. "You looked so beautiful, Lizzie—your cheeks flushed, red like your roses; I've never seen you look so beautiful. Lizzie with a gun in her hands! You were splendid! So brave and bold! Darling, don't you know, I love every part of you from the tips of the fingers to the toes! I don't want to make you suffer, sweetheart; on the contrary—I wanted you to be happy, so happy. I'd prepared this delicious meal for us, splurged; laid it all out in the dining room, put out all the best silver, the linen cloth, the napkins, Russian caviar, champagne, blinis with smoked salmon—all your favorite food. I was just opening the door to the back-yard."

Lizzie can imagine the feast he would have been capable of providing so thoughtfully and with so much good taste, the French windows open, the sunlight from the backyard shining on the silver.

She just looks at him, his unshaven face, the dark circles under his eyes, his obvious distress. She says, "But that's not what *I* saw when I came in the door!"

Sergei explains, "And then, unexpectedly, poor Martine rang the bell. I thought it was you—that you had forgotten your key. So I opened the door without looking to see who was there."

"And so! Did you have to sweep her up into your arms, em-brace her? Why didn't you just send her packing?" Lizzie asks angrily, picking up fistfuls of sand, letting the grains trickle through her fingers.

"She has a crush on me—and I hadn't seen her for ages! I have no idea why she took it into her head to come by and just ring my doorbell. I didn't know how to get rid of her, and I didn't have it in me to say anything hurtful—she's so young, so vulnerable, so much in love. You can imagine how she feels, no?"

"I certainly can!" Lizzie says, glaring at him.

"So I . . . well you saw what I did. It seemed the kindest way. And then as luck would have it, you came breezing in early. I was just trying to be gracious, to usher her out without hurting her. I don't want to make anyone suffer, you see—that's the problem."

Lizzie just looks at him hard, pursing her lips. "Sounds good," she says.

He looks up and down the beach, casting about, she can see, to change the subject, brushing the sand from his hands, his hair, and saying, "I don't want to fight, Lizzie. We're here together! I came racing out here this morning at the crack of dawn. We are so lucky to have one another—to both be alive, well, here, on this beautiful sunny fall Saturday. I got up at dawn just so we could spend the whole weekend together. Here we are on this beautiful beach, with the sea, the sky, the sun, all for us." He opens his long arms to the expanse of the beach and the pale sky.

"How long do you think we will be together just you and me? How will I feel when you go off again?" Lizzie says, looking hard at him, plucking at the blond blades of grass that thrust up from the dunes.

"We have known each other such a long time, Lizzie. Why would I ever leave you now?"

"Since the Hermitage," Lizzie says, smiling as their first meeting comes back so clearly. She remembers that time of hope in her life, her tumultuous stay in Russia in the 1990s when she first met Sergei, when things seemed to be changing all around her, when she believed she had fallen in love with the Russian language, Russian literature, Russian painting, with Russia, where democracy seemed to be blooming like her love for Sergei.

She and several of her Harvard friends were in Saint Petersburg on a summer semester abroad. They were visiting the Hermitage, the great museum. She sees the crowded rooms with all the famous paintings, remembers the musty smell, the large women guards sitting glumly against the walls.

She says, "I remember how we all used to laugh and say we could only find white things to eat in Russia: white cheese, white bread, yogurt, potatoes. You were wearing a shiny gray suit. I thought you looked so smart!"

"I was back there on business. Opportunities were opening up in an amazing way," Sergei says.

Lizzie gazes out at the sea and the sky, but she is back in the Hermitage staring at Sergei. "I was gazing at that painting—do you remember?" she says. "A beautiful Vermeer—*The Love Letter*. Wasn't it?"

"Lizzie! How could I forget?"

She goes on, "I remember it all so clearly. When you look at the painting you sort of feel you are looking through a keyhole at a maid who is giving a seated woman a letter. You came up and just stood there staring at me—looking down, I thought, at my legs; I must have had a short skirt on."

"Shorts, you had on shorts with dark sheer stockings underneath, and little boots—very American, very sexy."

"I thought you were admiring me, my legs, when you sidled up and whispered something in my ear. At first I couldn't hear what you said; then I realized what you were telling me!"

"What was I telling you?"

"That I had a hole in my stocking!"

"I never did! Would never! I was looking at your legs—maybe I pretended to see a hole in your stocking!"

"I had to laugh. A hole in my stocking! I did have a hole in my stocking; probably had several. Holes in my shoes! A starving student, trying to learn Russian."

"I invited you and your friends to dinner," Sergei says.

"You took us all to a big festive dinner in a fancy restaurant, and you told me to change my stockings first! 'You must change your stockings,' you said." Lizzie imitates his Russian accent, his deep voice, and laughs.

"I did not! Change your stockings! Never!" Sergei protests, but he is laughing, and Lizzie is sure it happened.

"We went to this grand place with dark paneled walls where they were playing balalaikas and singing sad songs," she says.

Sergei interrupts, "And where there was good Russian food— not white; delicious dark borscht, with lots of meat in it, piroshki, cutlets à la Kiev."

"There were so many interesting people there, and I was wowed—but even then you had a dark sophisticated girlfriend— or was it that man you were with? Was he a boyfriend?" Lizzie asks.

He shrugs. "Might have been someone, but when I saw you, whoever it was was immediately forgotten. I could tell right away how intelligent you were."

Lizzie adds, "We were in a crowd of young painters and writers, remember? Everyone speaking Russian, or trying to, and you were so much older, much more sophisticated."

"It was all so amazing. Russia, suddenly there was a frenzy of freedom, money; anything seemed possible, particularly when I said I was coming from New York—with my Russian surname I was golden."

"You knew everyone and you were so helpful, generous, you even found me a gallery owner in New York who wanted to put one of my paintings in a group show, irresistible. You were so encouraging—more than encouraging, helpful, but always with an eye out for someone else," Lizzie says.

"With an eye out for you, Lizzie. I wanted to be with you,

protect you, help you with your work!" Sergei protests, and she remembers how the two of them took the train to Moscow together, because he wanted to show her where he had been a boy. He took her through the streets, the web of little lanes where he had played, the arches and houses that had existed before Soviet times. He showed her the courtyards and even the old metro stations, though he kept saying how much it had all changed. He wanted her to see the buildings his parents told him about, where almost every family had had someone arrested during Stalin's reign.

Sergei says, "You told me how your mother had died so young and how Alice had brought you up—your father had moved into the country house and how you had been so lonely, vulnerable, poor, like me." He adds, "Why don't we plan a holiday, Lizzie? Just you and me. I could get away for a few weeks, maybe in December. Escape winter. Would you come?'

"Maybe," she says, turning her head, looking up at him, considering.

"Let's go somewhere splendid this winter, somewhere warm and wonderful, all my treat." He turns and nuzzles her neck.

Lizzie imagines it—the warm, calm Caribbean; a whitewashed hotel room with a terrace looking onto the sea; long, lazy days of room service with a flower on the tray; sex in the hot afternoons, Sergei's lithe body sticky with desire close beside her, his hands on her skin; not having to get up every morning at six to paint before heading out to teach in the gray and the winter's cold. How long will she be able to do that?

"Nothing else matters. Seize the day! Who knows what

tomorrow might bring? Look at your poor sister! Look what has happened to her out of the blue!"

"I know. All alone!" Lizzie says, the tears coming to her eyes.

"I feel for her. How will she go on alone without Michel? He loved her so much, took care of everything: that beautiful villa, the staff, Pamela—what a wonderful father, so devoted. Always at her side. He organized Alice's concerts, invited colleagues, people who came to hear her. He was just such a good, kind, loving husband and father."

Lizzie looks at Sergei sitting beside her, his aristocratic profile, chin tilted toward the sun, his long arms hugging his long legs, his elegant brown moccasins with the tassels. He speaks with so much sincere emotion and sympathy for her sister, she cannot help being moved.

"I can't believe he's gone," he says. "Is it possible that Michel who was such an expert sailor, a terrific swimmer, could have drowned like that in waters he knew so well, a boat he could handle so expertly, because of a few gusts of wind? Do you think he really wanted to kill himself?"

Lizzie says, "He always said that if he were to die he would like to do it in his boat—just drift out to sea. And I think he was having trouble at work—he had lost several clients recently. I'm not sure why or how but I know Alice was worried. Then there was the story about his father."

"What story?"

"Alice hinted once that his father was so distraught over his losses when he left Algeria and could not remake his fortune in France that he took his own life," Lizzie says.

Sergei says nothing, just staring at the sea.

Lizzie says, "Sometimes these things run in families."

"He never struck me as someone who would do something like that. There was something almost relentlessly optimistic about him. That's why he was so good at his job. Banks make money out of optimism. He always saw the silver lining, literally. Besides, there was Pamela. He loved her too much. Surely a father would never hurt his own child."

"Yet it happens," Lizzie says. "Though, it's true in his case it does not seem likely to me either. Poor little Pamela! She must be so sad. I hope she has good friends at school."

Sergei says, "I know things were difficult for him financially at the moment. All the Swiss banks, particularly the medium-sized private banks, have lost clients. They have all had to cut back, with all the publicity, the leaks of names, but still he had his job as far as I know. Did Alice say they wanted to fire him?"

"No, no, not as far as I know. He had been at that bank for many years; he knew all the top people well. There was according to Alice an unusual esprit de corps. I think he had been promoted because of all the people he knew, and it wasn't one of those banks with a high turnover, or a cutthroat atmosphere, though Alice always said he should never have been a banker, that he was not particularly good with figures or even computers."

"They valued him because of his charm, because everyone liked him, trusted him," Sergei says. "Most of the salespeople in those banks have no idea what they are selling. In fact the internal management often has no idea what's going on—it has all become far too complicated for the average person to understand.

Most of these bankers never say something is right or wrong; they speak in probabilities, or they should."

Lizzie nods, adding, "Well, he spoke so many languages, knew so many people—always said the right thing. Never judged. Everyone was at ease with him. It was a great gift. He made people laugh."

"I know. Actually I always thought Alice was rather hard on him. She underestimated him. Bossed him around, and was always making fun of him. I don't think she thought he was the sharpest arrow in the quiver," Sergei says, plucking at a piece of grass growing in the dunes.

"Oh! That's not fair!" Lizzie says. "On the contrary, she thought his intelligence might be better used in another perhaps more stimulating field."

"Well, listen, we can't all be artists. I'll admit Alice was probably smarter than Michel. She was probably a better judge of character, too. In some ways he was such an innocent, a Boy Scout. I'm not sure he was always aware of exactly what was going on. Some of the types he was mixed up with may have turned out to be unworthy of his trust. I remember him saying something recently on the telephone, sounding really angry, something like, 'Don't ever trust anyone completely.' It sounded as if someone had let him down."

"Well, I'm sure it wasn't Alice. True, she can be ironic, and perhaps he didn't always appreciate her caustic sense of humor—people don't always understand our particular sense of humor. Humor does not translate well. But Alice loved him so much. She was undone when he died! Last night when we went to the restaurant, she was weeping. I've never seen Alice weep like that. She's such a stalwart soul. Someone of real integrity," Lizzie says.

"I suppose she did love him, but apparently she was not always generous with her favors. We discussed it once out on his boat, and I remember him telling me that she would say, 'Everything comes to those who wait.'"

"Oh! That's so unfair!" Lizzie says again. "Alice loved Michel." She boxes Sergei on his arm.

"Still, did she admire him, desire him? After all, he was the one paying the bills. Really, what she didn't understand was that he *was* a good businessman, a good banker in his own way—or anyway an absolutely honest one. He didn't understand dishonesty. There was a code he followed absolutely obstinately."

"How do you know?" Lizzie asks, turning her head to look at Sergei, who puts his hand to his unshaven cheek.

"He did some business for me, actually—and he was always so fair, scrupulously honest. I made some money with him—quite a bit, actually. Introduced him to some Russian colleagues, business partners in the real estate firm, and everyone loved him and thought he was such a great guy."

Lizzie says, "I didn't know you did business with Michel. You never told me that!"

He looks at her, shrugs, and says, "Well, it was not the sort of thing one advertised, and Michel was very discreet—a banker of the old-fashioned kind."

Lizzie looks at Sergei, a thought coming suddenly to her mind. "Do you think there might have been some sort of foul play?" she asks, wondering suddenly if there might have been someone else with Michel on the boat, someone dangerous.

Sergei looks at her with a grin and a glimmer of aggression, a hard glint in his eye. "You have murder on the mind, Miss Lizzie!"

She says, "*Honestly* I didn't think it was loaded—it looked like something in a museum, such an ancient, heavy old weapon."

"*I* didn't know it was loaded either! But you picked it up and fired at me!"

"Well, I didn't think at all, to tell you the truth. I just opened the drawer and there it was."

"You knew it was there! I had shown it to you once."

Lizzie says, "I just grabbed it, squeezed, and the trigger gave. It—it went off mechanically. I wasn't really thinking or looking at you or anything. All I remember is thinking that your words seemed like stones thrown at me, and I had to stop you from throwing them." She remembers it happening by chance, an accident. "Though I'll admit there was a moment, when I held it in my hand, the weight of it."

Sergei thrusts her back down into the sand half playfully. He rolls on top of her and holds her down by her shoulders when she tries to free herself, his long hard body against hers. "A moment when you saw me dead and liked the idea, no? A sort of jubilation! Hurrah! Hurrah! He's dead! Finally! No? You probably found it exciting! Didn't you? Admit! Oh!"

"I did not! Let me go! You are hurting me," she says. He is holding her now too tightly by her wrists, and though he is laughing, she catches a glint of something cold and hard in his hazel eyes.

"You even find the thought of it exciting now, don't you? The thought of my death! Admit it!"

"I do not!" she protests, but more feebly. "Let me go!"

"I'm going to tell the police unless . . ."

"Unless what? Let me go! You are hurting me!"

2

They come back down the driveway that afternoon, passing under the magnolia tree. Lizzie half expects Alice to be standing in the bright September light on the doorstep waiting, her hand to her forehead, an apron around her waist. When Alice and Lizzie lived together in New York, Alice was the one who did all the cooking, took care of the house, kept everything tidy.

Now Lizzie and Sergei walk down the path toward the blue door, holding hands and gaily swinging the bags with groceries Sergei has bought. Lizzie stops to wave at the kitchen windows, where she thinks she catches a glimmer of Alice's face. She calls out, "We've got food!" but there is no response.

Instead, all is dead quiet and cool in the house. On the kitchen table Lizzie finds a scribbled note on a yellow piece of paper under a glass. She can hardly read the scrawled words Alice has written in obvious haste: "Tried to call you. Gone to catch plane for Zurich. Pamela gone. Will call as soon as I have news." Under the note there is some money with a P.S. telling Lizzie to get Rosa to come and tidy the house.

Sergei puts the bag of groceries on the kitchen table and asks, "What's happened?"

Lizzie holds the note in her trembling hands and says, "Alice has gone to Switzerland."

"What? Where? Why?" Sergei asks, as Lizzie gives him the note to read.

Lizzie says, "Why didn't she wait for us? I would have gone with her at least back to the airport. I would even have caught the plane with her. I wish I'd taken my cell phone with me to the beach!"

"How could this have happened?" Sergei asks, looking suddenly pale. He takes out his cell phone from his back pocket, looking down at his messages.

Lizzie leans on the back of one of the painted kitchen chairs to steady her spinning head. The whole house seems empty and silent and cold.

Lizzie immediately misses Alice with a dull ache. It feels like the first time Alice left home, and Lizzie had to cope on her own, when Alice was in her junior year at Barnard and went abroad for a semester to Paris. Lizzie has been so looking forward to spending some time with her sister, talking to her, confiding in her, asking for her sisterly advice. Now she has gone.

"How do you think she found out?" Sergei asks.

"Suppose they must have called from her school sometime after we left—oh, God, poor Alice; she must be in such a state!"

"We have to find out what happened," he says, standing in the doorway leaning his lithe hip against the jamb, holding his phone and looking at Lizzie.

"You read the note. All she says is that Pamela has disappeared. It must have been early this morning—they are five or six hours ahead of us, of course. She must have disappeared after breakfast, or sometime early this morning. Suppose they must have called here looking for her mother. Alice would have left the house phone number as well as her cell to call in case of an emergency."

"Why on earth did Alice send the girl back to boarding school?" Sergei asks.

"Apparently that's where she wanted to be—at school, with her friends. Understandable, I guess, at that age." She adds, "I think it was Djamilla who persuaded Alice to let her go."

"Djamilla?"

"Poor little Pamela!" Lizzie says. "What could be going through her mind? What are we going to do?" Her eyes are filled with tears, her wrists ache, and she feels faint. "It's all so awful."

"I'll make some calls. See what I can find out," Sergei says. "Djamilla might know something. She always seemed to know everything. Where has she gone, anyway? Did Alice say? Could Pamela have gone to her? She loved her."

Lizzie shakes her head. "According to Alice she, too, seems to have sort of disappeared. She might have gone back to Algeria, to her family. I think she came from Oran—I remember her once telling me."

Lizzie remembers the elderly woman with her slippers that made a shuffling noise as she came down the red-tiled corridor in the villa, in her black head scarf, the long dress. "Remember last summer, when we were in Beaulieu-sur-Mer, we found her looking through our things?" She recalls opening the door and seeing the woman standing there in the guest room looking at something in her hand. She startled and put it down on the desk.

"I knew someone had been through my clothes and rearranged things and at first I thought she was just particularly diligent, looking for laundry, or wanted to help tidy up, but then I found her looking at a receipt from my pocket."

"She was a terrible snoop. If anyone knows what happened to Michel I bet she would," Sergei says.

"Did Michel ever mention Luigi?"

They look at each other.

"Luigi? The graduate student who was staying in my house? What does he have to do with this?" Sergei asks.

Lizzie looks away and says, "That's for Alice to know and for Alice to tell." Sergei leaves the room with his cell phone in hand.

She opens the door to speak to Sergei but he waves a hand, speaking in fast Russian, and goes into the bathroom and closes the door.

PART VII

AMAGANSETT

Saturday Afternoon

I

ᴌIZZIE

1

That afternoon someone comes to pick Sergei up—a colleague, he tells Lizzie—and he goes into East Hampton on business, leaving Lizzie to her work. She sits upstairs in the small bedroom at the wooden desk along the wall, her mother's old English desk with the drop-down top and the pigeonholes for letters. She is trying to correct papers for the three basic art history classes she is teaching once again this fall at Brooklyn College, but she cannot concentrate. She has to teach a heavy load, which does not allow her any time for her own work. She is working on a big, ambitious abstract painting with bright colors, and she needs time to finish it.

She has installed herself up here for a few hours with her sketchbook, her crayons, her computer, and her small turquoise suitcase, which lies open on the floor beside her, some of her belongings scattered across the bed. Lizzie has never learned to be tidy, living mostly on her own or with her sister, who would tidy up for her. She and Alice lived together in the Village in a studio with a loft, which they built themselves, but when that became too expensive for Lizzie on her own she rented a smaller space in Park Slope in Brooklyn, where she teaches. It is one of the advantages of living alone, she thinks: you can leave your things lying around. She knows her untidiness bothers Sergei, who likes order.

Lizzie thinks of the first time Alice left home and she had to cope on her own. Alice went abroad for a semester to the Sorbonne in Paris when Lizzie was just fourteen, still at the Quaker school in New York. It was there that Alice met Michel, who was studying in Paris at Sciences Politiques, though they did not marry until later. Alice initially resisted Michel's advances. Though she was immediately attracted to him, she hesitated to marry him. She found him, she told Lizzie, too polite, too kind, too inoffensive, too easily influenced. She said he was like a blank slate, tabula rasa; he wanted to be absolutely everyone's best friend, always agreeing with everything everyone said, which she felt must be a cover for something more sinister. "He's a crowd of variations," she told Lizzie, who had gone over to join Alice for her summer vacation. Lizzie liked him immediately and said, "If you don't marry him I will, when I'm old enough. He's adorable."

Lizzie has been so looking forward to asking Alice for her sisterly advice. What should she do about Sergei? Should she trust him? Give him an ultimatum? She once saw a therapist who suggested that Sergei's drives were confused, that he seemed uncertain, always moving from woman to woman or even to a man. Did he see no distinction? Soon she will be too old to have children of her own. Should she give up that opportunity to be with a man whom she can see only infrequently, fascinating though he may be? There is no one she can talk to about this.

She guiltily thought that now, without Michel, she could have Alice all to herself again, at least for a while. She imagined it would be as it had been before when they were girls, when Alice would listen for hours to Lizzie talking about her life. Now she is gone again and for an indefinite time and in such great distress. Lizzie tries once more to call her on her cell phone, but she must already be on the plane or perhaps in a line at the airport where she has had to turn off her phone, as there is no reply.

She wonders if Alice has had any news about Pamela and where she might be. What could have happened to her? Alice said Pamela had so desperately wanted to be back at school with her friends and teachers, yet once there, she seems to have run away again. Perhaps the reality did not turn out to be what she had expected. But where could she have gone? Does she perhaps have friends in the town? Even a boyfriend, though she is so young? Lizzie remembers having a first crush, what she took for love for a young boy with wonderful blond curly hair whom she had met at the Quaker school, which they had both attended when she was only twelve and he not much older. But why would Pamela not have let her mother know where she was?

Alice is the one who has always been so fair, able to see things from another's point of view. Lizzie has always felt close to her sister, who stepped in so bravely when their mother died, though Alice was only twelve years old and Lizzie barely five. Now Alice is forty-two and Lizzie thirty-five. She remembers how Alice would try to sing her the same songs their mother had, not always remembering all the words.

Lizzie looks through her old big untidy handbag, as though she might find some answers there. She takes out her small leather agenda, which Alice gave her years ago. She flips through the pages, sees the entries for this past March, which Alice spent with her in Italy. She opens up her ancient black wallet and finds some bills that Alice must have stuffed in there, knowing she needs money. She discovers several hundred-dollar bills, to her surprise, tears coming to her eyes.

She wonders uneasily about the large sums of insurance money that Alice seems to have acquired as a result of Michel's death. Why would he have doubled the insurance suddenly, at such a moment in midlife and in good health? He had never seemed like a depressive man to her. What could have caused such despair?

2

Lizzie remembers the most recent spring vacation in Italy. She was staying in one of Sergei's villas in the countryside near Rome. Sergei, who as a child had lived in a crowded two-room Soviet apartment with his parents, his grandparents, and an unmarried aunt who insisted on keeping a few chickens on the balcony, had always longed for space of his own, he had told her. He has obviously done very well in real estate, and has acquired a string of houses and apartments all over the world, including one in Mexico City, an apartment in London, a chalet in Saint Moritz, and the villa in Italy, which he likes to lend.

While away in Siberia on business, Sergei had called Lizzie one night and told her she could have his fifteenth-century villa in the Roman countryside.

"Stay in my house. Best time of year to be there. Not too hot or cold. Not too many tourists in Rome. I don't like empty houses, wasted spaces. I'd like to think of you there, keeping it warm for me, enjoying the view of the Roman hills. You could get some work done, set up your easel in the garden or one of the rooms. It's a perfect place for a painter, in a very quiet area. If you want company ask your sister to come, too. Big old rambling house, umpteen rooms—somewhat in want of repair, but so beautiful," Sergei had said.

She had been tempted by the thought of Rome, the paintings she could look at there, the quiet of the countryside, a whole house to herself.

When Lizzie arrived at the villa on a bright afternoon, she found the key where Sergei had told her it would be: under a terra-cotta flowerpot with white narcissi bowing their heads by the front door. In the entrance hall, she put down her small suitcase and wandered through the cool high-ceilinged rooms, which were shuttered against the sunlight, listening to the sound of her footsteps. She had the feeling of stepping back in time in this strange ancient house with its thick walls, its long-stemmed pine trees and olive groves, all of which unexpectedly seemed familiar to her. She felt she had been here before, in some other life or in a dream.

She had assumed the house was completely empty and was surprised and somewhat disconcerted when she walked into the big kitchen, with its rafters and red-tiled floor and even a chicken strutting about, to find a thin olive-skinned cook in a gray uniform and white apron who had a squint in one eye and smiled at her while standing over the sink washing dishes. She dried her hands on her apron and introduced herself in Italian as Rosario, and immediately asked what Lizzie would like for dinner, as though that was the most important thing in the world. When Lizzie smiled and thanked her in her rudimentary Italian and said she had not yet considered the matter, the cook proposed pasta alla puttanesca, enumerating the ingredients at length for Lizzie: capers, olives, and tomatoes, a local dish that she said Lizzie was bound to enjoy.

In the big dining room with the windows that opened onto the garden with its lemon trees in wooden boxes, a young blond housekeeper with a crimson ribbon in her hair was polishing the dining table energetically.

Then faintly, in the distance, Lizzie heard a piano playing. Was Sergei here after all, she thought for one wild moment, following the sound of the notes. She knew he played the piano well. She walked quickly, following the music, which she recognized like a familiar language, a lovely Schubert piece that her father would play for his girls in the evenings. Those were the moments when she had felt closest to him, listening to him play and watching his beautiful hands, which he lifted from the keys slowly and graciously. She would notice the way he swayed back and forth, his feet pumping the pedals in his old narrow shoes.

Lizzie is not musical, but she has always enjoyed listening to both her father and Alice play. She walked down the corridor, imagining she might find her father's ghost here in this strange

Roman house. She passed several shuttered rooms and came into a book-lined study, where she found not her father or Sergei, but a stranger, a handsome man with dark hair falling on his forehead. He was dressed entirely in black—black jeans, black T-shirt, black cardigan—and was playing the old grand piano, which stood before an open window.

He looked up at her as she stopped still in the doorway, taking his white long-fingered hands from the keys with a flourish, the way her father would. He stared at her and got up, a flush rising in his cheeks. He introduced himself and explained he was a graduate student; he spoke very good English. He said he was working on organizing Sergei's library and his papers and staying in his study. He waved a hand at the striped sofa bed. "Very comfortable," he said with a quick smile. Lizzie was not sure what to make of all of that. Why had Sergei not mentioned him?

He seemed to know vaguely who she was.

"You are a painter?" he asked, and she nodded and for some reason felt obliged to add, "Not very well known! I've only had a few shows, mostly in groups. I have to do a lot of teaching, too."

Luigi shrugged his shoulders and lifted his hands elegantly, as if fame were a woman he knew well and had spurned. "I'm not sure that fame is a good thing."

Then he asked if he would be in the way, adding that Sergei had left an old car and that he would be happy to drive her around if she wished to see the countryside. "No, of course not," Lizzie felt obliged to say, though his presence did seem awkward to her, and she had no wish to go anywhere. What she wanted most of all at that moment was to stay just where she was, before the open window with the sound of cicadas and the smell of sunlight coming to her.

Was she supposed to treat Luigi like an employee and ignore him, or was she supposed to invite him to have meals with her? She had been hoping to have her days to herself, to get some of her own work done in the quiet and solitude of the house. Her vacations were so precious to her, rare moments when she could concentrate on her own projects. She knew the house was large and the grounds seemed endless—there was certainly room for them both—but she wondered if it would be awkward. When she asked, he said he had been here for months. Lizzie wondered if Sergei had even remembered that Luigi was still here and what he was supposedly doing for him. Organizing his library? Did he have so many books? Cataloguing papers?

The villa was on the side of a hill, not far from Rome, with, as Sergei had told her, a beautiful view of the hills and in the distance the sea. When Lizzie had installed herself in one of the smaller guest bedrooms in the back, she had a sudden thought that seemed brilliant at the time. She decided to call Alice and ask if she would like to join her for a few days. It would make things less awkward, she felt, to have her older sister with her, and it might be a way to reciprocate Alice's grand hospitality. Lizzie had spent so many summers with her and Michel in Beaulieu-sur-mer.

"Come and stay. It's so beautiful here. I'm all on my own in the middle of the Roman countryside. Well, alone, that is, apart from a whole willing staff here—cook, maid, who wants to wash my clothes, and even a sort of secretary with a car who is dying to drive someone around. Can you come?" she asked Alice.

"Where's Sergei?" Alice asked.

"I believe he's in Siberia," Lizzie said. Sergei seemed to go often to Siberia, which he said was a place of grand opportunities—rather like the West had once been in America. He wanted to take her there one day.

So Alice consented to come for a few days. Luigi offered to get her at the airport in Rome, to pick her up in Sergei's old, beat-up silver Jeep. Lizzie was working hard on a big painting in the garden, which was going well, and let Luigi pick her older sister up. She has never really liked to drive—she always loses her way—and particularly not in Italy.

When Alice arrived she looked pink-cheeked and pleased to be with Lizzie in this lovely place. "But it's beautiful here! What a treat!" she said as Luigi showed her around the lovely old villa as though he owned it.

Later, he offered to chauffeur Alice around the Roman countryside, and Lizzie said it might be a good idea. It would be something pleasant for Alice to do, she surmised. Sergei had left the old Jeep for them to use, apparently, and Luigi was very knowledgeable about the history of the Roman countryside. He had been born in Rome, belonged to an ancient Roman family, even worked as a papal guard in the Vatican on Sundays in his black suit. He knew the area well.

So, obligingly, he drove Alice, who did not know Rome well. They went into the city and also visited Hadrian's Villa in Tivoli, and even went as far as Florence and Pisa. Sometimes they stayed overnight in an inn in one of the towns.

When they came back late in the evening, Lizzie felt obliged to ask Luigi to join them for dinner. The three of them ate the delicious local dishes that Rosario prepared from them. They sat out on the terrace overlooking the hills on fine evenings. Then, one evening, Luigi mentioned that he loved music and would like to hear Alice play.

Lizzie said, "Luigi plays the piano very well himself." He begged Alice to play her violin, which she consented to do if he played with her. Alice and Luigi ended up playing a difficult Beethoven violin sonata together, while Lizzie sat on the sofa bed in the study sipping Sergei's old cognac, listening to the lovely music and wishing he were with them. Day after day, Alice prolonged her stay for the entire two weeks that Lizzie spent in the house.

Lizzie remembers it as a happy time when she was free to work and to walk in the cool, shady gardens under the pines, the olives, and the lemon trees with her sister. She had never seen Alice so happy, nor had she ever heard her play so well. She remembers how the old house was always filled with music—or so it seemed to her. Alice was full of energy, up early in the morning practicing her violin. Then she would go off with Luigi touring the countryside in the afternoons. Lizzie can see her now, standing at the window of Sergei's study, with her violin and bow in hand, her head back, her dark hair falling smoothly from her lovely face.

In the evenings Alice and Luigi would come back dusty and disheveled and famished. Together, they would all eat dinner, great heaps of pasta in various sauces, on the terrace and drink Sergei's good wine. They felt his permissive presence hovering over them benevolently. Everything seemed possible. Often when Rosario had finished making something delicious she would stand at the side of the table on the terrace and join in the Italian conversation—both Lizzie and Alice spoke some rudimentary Italian. Rosario spoke of Sergei with words of high praise. "*Un signore!*" she would say with admiration, opening up her arms to convey something expansive.

Luigi would nod and agree and tell some anecdote commending Sergei's kindness, his generosity. Apparently Sergei had paid for his graduate studies in music at the university in Rome. Sergei rewarded his staff well for their services, Lizzie thought. He called from time to time and seemed delighted the three of them were together in the house.

"Help yourselves to anything you want," he said. "Enjoy the books, the piano, the view, the car."

This went on until Michel called and told Alice she must come home immediately. "He sounds very upset. I've never heard him sound so angry," Alice said, looking worried. She packed her suitcase immediately and left in haste the next day.

Had Michel somehow discovered Alice's betrayal? Had she really betrayed him? What was her relationship with Luigi, then? Lizzie had never questioned it before, always relying on her sister's probity, her honesty, her love for Michel, but she was perhaps mistaken. It was true that Alice had seemed transformed during those days, filled with energy, her fine face lit up, her skin shining, her magical music filling the old rooms as if with bright flowers.

PART VIII

SWITZERLAND

Saturday and Sunday

I

PAMELA

1

Early Saturday morning, right after breakfast, when everyone else has to go to a special lecture on the environment and the conservation of energy, which sounds boring to Pamela, she decides to stay in the garden. It is such a sunny day, the light so bright, the sky a pale blue. No one seems to mind. She descends the stone steps and goes into the sunken garden on her own. The birds are singing fiercely, the sun is shining so brightly, and she is thinking about her father, imagining him coming to find her, so she does not hear the man approach—or if she does she imagines it might be her father.

She is sitting on the bench, just staring at the silver leaves trembling in the light, when the man comes up to her. She notices his thick neck and broad shoulders. She thinks he might be a new gym teacher or a secretary or even a parent who has come to visit and entered the school grounds by mistake at the side gate. The moment seems not quite real to her, like something happening to another girl sitting in the school garden, seen from afar.

Then she sees what he has in his hand, but even then she feels there has been some sort of mistake. He says, "Pamela?" as if he knows her, and she wonders if he is some relative or friend of her father's she has forgotten about, and why he would be carrying a gun. She keeps thinking this is not quite real, that there has been some error that will be explained.

Perhaps he is some sort of school detective. She stands up politely and nods her head, and such is her training that even despite the gun she makes a half movement to shake his hand.

Then he says softly and with an accent that she recognizes as Russian, "Come with me, please. If you come quietly no one will be hurt." Then she understands what is happening, unbelievable though it might be. She feels rather like an actress in a play, and wonders what will happen next.

She casts a furtive glance around the garden, but there is no one in sight. All the students are in the lecture by now and the teachers either still in their rooms or in their common room having coffee or chatting with one another at this early hour. So she goes obediently down the narrow path, which he indicates with a slight nod of his head, going through the bushes and under the trees to the side gate, which the man must have come through and has obviously left open. Even as she goes, she is still not quite certain what this man wants of her. Perhaps this is some kind of a joke.

Outside in the street when she sees his shiny black car, she finally understands. Then she wants to turn back and run, but it is too late.

He tells her to get into the back of the car, and for a moment she hesitates, looking around for help. She wants to cry out, but there is no one in the street at that early hour. The man puts the gun on the roof of the car, takes something from his pocket, and ties her hands behind her back so fast she cannot resist. She watches herself from afar, a young girl in a green pleated school skirt and lace-ups and a man in a gray hat who whips out a dark cloth that he pulls tightly over her face. She is plunged into sudden darkness, trussed and bound, like a captured animal. She hears him open the rear door of the car, and he pushes her roughly inside.

She hears the front door of the car open and the engine start up, and he drives off. "Lie down," he says when she tries, at last, to scream, "No! Please!" She thinks of her mother and sees her standing before the window, head back, elbow lifted, playing her violin.

II

ALICE

1

When Alice finally arrives in Zurich, it is early Sunday morning, though for her it is still the middle of Saturday night. She was not able to sleep a single moment on the plane, thinking of Pamela, unable to read even the headlines of the newspaper she had grabbed on departure. On the plane, in the silent darkness with the green light of the lamp lit above her, she thought only of Pamela. She imagined she was trying to reach her and could not for some reason. Surely she would have called to let her know she was leaving her school. Why this unbearable silence? Nothing worse than silence, Alice thought, because one can fill it with one's worst imaginings. It seemed impossible to Alice that Pamela would be so cruel as to purposefully leave her mother in such suspense. She is a determined child with a mind of her own, but not a cruel one. She remembered Pamela once as a little girl just marching off down the road in a rage, her school backpack on her back, her thick plaits with their big bows bouncing behind her. Was she angry with her mother? she wondered. Or just with life, which must seem so unfair? Children, Alice feels, are acutely aware of injustice. Was it possible Pamela felt Alice was in some way responsible for her father's death?

On arrival, Alice takes a taxi in the gray early morning light, going to the hotel she has booked for a night in the city. She goes up to her room, thinking of her sister and wishing she had waited and asked Lizzie to come with her. She misses her and feels now unbearably tired and terrified, as though she has been traveling through the night forever.

She immediately calls Pamela's school and asks to speak to the headmaster, Mr. Burns, and after an unbearable wait of several minutes—is the man actually still in his bed?—he finally answers the phone. "Ah! Madame de Sevigné, I'm so glad to hear from you. Is Pamela all right?" The headmaster sounds relieved, as though Alice has the answers to any questions he might have about her daughter.

"I have traveled through the night and am now at a hotel in Zurich in order to answer that question. Have you not had any news?" she asks the man.

"Us? No, no, I'm afraid not. We thought Pamela would have contacted you by now. We presumed she had decided to go home or perhaps rather to follow you to America, which seemed natural to us. We thought she had had a change of mind and decided to go to you there. Are you sure she's not on her way to America? Perhaps you two have passed one another like ships in the night?" Mr. Burns says with a little laugh and rather slowly, almost as if he has something in his mouth. *Is this heartless man actually eating his breakfast, chomping on a piece of toast, while he laughs about my lost daughter?* Alice thinks indignantly.

She asks, "Have you notified the police?"

Mr. Burns says he did not think it was necessary.

"Sunday morning," he reminds her cheerfully, as if that has anything to do with it! He discussed the matter with the school psychologist, Pamela's teachers, and even some of her friends yesterday, and everyone felt sure she had simply decided she wanted to be with her family at a time like this, and had probably just left impulsively early yesterday morning, without telling anyone.

"The weekend, after all. Madame de Sevigné will remember that the students have the right to leave the school on weekends if they check out with Matron," he says.

"How on earth could she have done that?" Alice asks, exasperated by the man's calm.

"Or perhaps she simply needs some time on her own? Don't you think, madame? Such a competent girl and so grown-up for her age. So clever, our Pamela—I'm sure there's some logical explanation for her behavior," he says, as though he owned her.

"My daughter has now been missing for twenty-four hours and if I understand rightly, you have done nothing about it!" Alice shouts into the phone, her temples beating. "Pamela may be competent but she is only fourteen years old! She was in your care, after all. Why was she not with the other students? Where was she after breakfast? Didn't someone notice where she was? She could hardly have vanished into thin air. Why was there no supervision? Why was she allowed to wander around on her own? Who saw her last?"

"It was at breakfast, as I told you yesterday, that she was last seen here," Mr. Burns says. "According to her friends she ate well and seemed quite cheerful, but said she was going into the garden, as it was such a lovely day. We felt, as I said, that she might like a little time on her own after suffering such a traumatic loss. We did not oblige her to attend class or the special lectures we have on Saturday mornings—we had a wonderful lecture given by a distinguished professor on the environment and how to conserve energy, but it was after all a Saturday morning. We allowed dear Pamela, one of our most favorite students, a certain latitude, the freedom to roam in our beautiful, safe garden. We thought it might be soothing. Our intentions were certainly of the best!"

Alice retorts, "That may indeed be the case but surely you realize she has little or no money on her—and where could she have gone on her own? How could she have just taken a plane to America? Don't you think I would have notified you? Or she would have notified me first? Why would she not have told her teachers or her friends or informed her mother of her whereabouts? How could she have just disappeared like this?" She is getting angrier and angrier as she speaks. Shouting, she adds, "This is unconscionable!"

Mr. Burns says that they of course informed her the moment they realized Pamela was not at the school, but at the same time she must understand—as is becoming more and more apparent to Alice—that he has his school's considerable reputation, the good of *all* the students, to consider. Everything that could have been done for Pamela given the circumstances has been done. Everyone has been very sensitive to her situation. He asks

Alice if Pamela has any friends in the environs of the school. Could she have gone to visit someone she knew, and forgotten perhaps to check out with Matron? Did she perhaps know some young man to whom she might have had recourse at a time like this?

Alice can hardly contain her rage now. "Are you implying that my innocent fourteen-year-old daughter might be on an assignation of some kind? Are you implying she is some kind of whore?"

The headmaster immediately denies any such allegation. He says that of course if Alice feels this is a matter for the police, he will notify them immediately. He will do anything she thinks appropriate. He understands her concern, though it might be wiser to wait until tomorrow morning, Monday, and see if there is any word from Pamela. It is rather early now, on a Sunday morning.

Alice says, "My daughter is perhaps in great danger!" She tells him she expects him to call the police immediately, and slams down the phone.

III

$\mathcal{P}$AMELA

1

She is not sure afterward how long they have traveled.

She tries to make the man understand she is uncomfortable, but her moaning and attempts at speech have no effect at all. He ignores her and drives on relentlessly.

Muffled in the darkness, she has no idea where he is going, except that it seems to her that the road winds continuously and goes up and then down. She hears him shifting gears before a turn and then accelerating into the curve the way her father would do in his fast car. The farther they travel, the more terrified she becomes.

Her hands are tightly tied and they hurt, but her attempts to free them from the rope are in vain. She has to get out of this car. She is going farther and farther from safety, farther and farther from her mother, her aunt, her school, she thinks, her heart beating hard, saliva coming sickeningly into her mouth. The thick black cloth tied so closely over her face blinds her and makes her feel she cannot breathe. The man seems to be driving fast along this curving road, and she feels so sick. Lying down in the back of a car with no air makes her feel nauseated. She ate a big English breakfast of eggs and bacon and toast this morning at school, and she is afraid she might vomit into the tight gag and suffocate.

She tries to think of her mother, her father, and her aunt. Why didn't she stay with her mother? How could she have left her alone to make the trip to America? She wonders when her teachers will discover she is gone, and what her mother will do when they call her and she hears Pamela has disappeared. She imagines her mother's panic and shock. Will she come immediately to Switzerland, to the school, and will they call the police? But surely that would do no good. How could anyone find her? They cannot check every car on the road.

She needs to go to the bathroom badly, too. She drank a lot of tea at breakfast and a big glass of orange juice. Eventually and shamefully she crouches down in the back of the car and allows the warm urine to run down her legs, and seep into her pleated skirt and her socks.

2

Finally, after what seems to her many hours without stopping, the car slows and halts abruptly. She hears the man get out and open the back door. He reaches in and helps her out. He ushers her up some steps, the urine squelching now in her shoes. She's afraid she might vomit and swallows, her knees wavy, like water. Where is she? Where is he taking her? She hears him open a door, and he thrusts her inside. Then he takes the cloth off her face and unties her hands. She blinks, half-blind, standing in a large dark paneled hall. There are the antlers of a deer over a door, and a purple oriental carpet partly covering the shiny parquet floor. Several doors lead off the hall. The house must be large, the ceiling high. Stairs go up to a landing above.

The man with the thick neck, dark glasses, and hat opens one of the doors onto a small windowless bathroom and closes the door behind her. She sinks down gratefully to pee again. She gulps water from the tap and washes her face and hands with cold water and soap at the small clean basin. With a hand towel by the sink, she tries to sponge off her stained school skirt where the urine seeped through.

She looks at the strange gray face in the mirror, the big dark eyes wild with terror, the disheveled blond hair. She hardly recognizes this terrified girl who looks more like a frightened wild animal. She turns away and leans against the wall for a moment, trying to catch her breath, to regain some semblance of composure. She knows she has to try to be calm. She must watch and think clearly; she must make a plan.

When she emerges into the hall a matronly woman with smooth, creamy skin and a wart on her cheek, wearing a blue uniform and an apron and carrying some clean towels, is waiting for her. She ushers Pamela up the stairs and into a long corridor. At the end of the corridor she unlocks and opens a door to a bedroom and tells her she can go inside. "*Avanti*," she says, which Pamela knows is Italian. Is she in the Italian part of Switzerland? she wonders. She knows there is a French, a German, and an Italian part of Switzerland; she believes the Italian section is a southern region of the country. She was once on a business trip with her father to Lugano. She remembers a beautiful lake.

The maid puts the clean towels on the end of the bed and nods her head, and before Pamela has time to ask her where they are or why, she leaves her alone. Pamela hears the maid lock the door behind her.

She looks around. There is a four-poster bed with a blue-and-white-checked bedspread, a wooden bedside table with a porcelain lamp, and a desk in one corner. A comfortable room, she sees, with a thick gray carpet on the floor, and even a pink vase with artificial pink roses on the desk. The room is not that much different from her own at home, in Beaulieu-sur-Mer. She tells herself it is not a dank dungeon or a hole in the ground where she has to crouch, unable to stand up. Does that mean these people intend to keep her alive, to keep her here with them for a while? she wonders. There is even a tiny bathroom with a toilet, a shower, and a small window high above the toilet. Everything is clean, neat, polished, anonymous. No photographs, no books.

She wonders what these people want with her. Where is she? She looks out the window in the room and sees fir trees and in the distance the winding road, which must be the way they came here. She tries the window handle, but it is locked. If she could somehow get out the window, she thinks, she could probably climb down to the ground and then make her way to the road. Surely someone would pick her up and take her back to school. But could she make it to the road before someone stopped her? And if she goes back to her school they might come for her there again. She knows she has to get away from here.

There is a knock on the door, and the maid in the blue uniform comes in with some clean clothes for her: dry white socks, white cotton underpants, and a navy skirt. Pamela thanks the woman, who smiles not unkindly and replies, "*Prego,*" but she leaves the room again before Pamela can question her.

She tries on the clean clothes and finds that the navy blue skirt fits, though the underpants balloon around her legs. She wonders who wore these clothes before her, and where they came from.

PART IX

AMAGANSETT

Late Saturday Night

I

1

Lizzie lies next to Sergei in the double bed in the big bedroom, but she cannot sleep. The lined curtains are drawn in the dark and silent room where her parents slept, and where her father died. Though they lie with their limbs companionably entwined, Lizzie has not wanted to make love to Sergei. Her mind is not on love or desire, but on death: her mother's death when Lizzie was so young, and then her father's only a year ago. These ghosts have lingered on here with her in the old house. She has never been able to chase them away completely.

Now there is Michel's death and her own role in the tragedy. She thinks of Luigi and how Alice said to her one afternoon, giving her a kiss on her cheek, "How lovely of you to invite me here."

More and more it seems to her that this was not a natural death. This was no accident, but something prepared for, known in advance—Michel was too good a sailor, and why the increase in the insurance only weeks before his death?

She rises quietly, takes a blanket and her pillow, and goes down the stairs and out into the quiet living room, with its high ceiling and big windows, which let in the light of the moon. She settles down in the shadows of the old sofa, where she slept so soundly beside Alice only the night before.

Lizzie wonders where Alice is now and if she has arrived in Zurich yet and contacted the school. Is she lying alone in some hotel room?

At some point Sergei emerges from the bedroom, looking for her. "You can't sleep either?" she asks him as he walks over to her in his pajama top, which covers the essentials. He sits down beside her. "Move over," he says, and puts his arm around her shoulders.

"Were you worrying, too, about Pamela?" Lizzie asks.

He nods and says, "Such a bright, engaging kid."

"I know you are fond of her," she says, thinking that Sergei has always been kind and generous with Pamela, that he enjoys children. She wonders if he would make a good father. They sit side by side in the faint light of the moon.

"What on earth could have happened to her?" Lizzie asks eventually, sitting forward on the sofa. She is wearing an old frilly nylon nightgown, slightly yellowed around the boatneck, one she has found in the chest of drawers in the big bedroom; it must have belonged to their mother. They were never able to bring themselves to get rid of their mother's clothes, just using them when they were old enough to wear them. Sergei turns his head, looks at her, and sighs. He says, "I like you in that old nightgown," and puts his hand on her neck. She brushes it away.

Sergei says, "Look, Alice said Pamela wanted to go back to school to be with her friends, no? And perhaps things didn't plan out as she expected, and she must have run away."

Lizzie says, "But she's not that impulsive. I can't see her running away. And where would she have run to? Surely there was some kind of supervision in a school of that kind."

"Perhaps not—one of those posh Swiss schools filled mostly with rich, spoiled foreign kids, where they can do pretty much what they like, no?" Sergei says.

"Just pray she's not in danger of some kind."

"Why would she be?" he asks, looking around the room and muttering, as if speaking to himself.

Turning to look at him sharply, Lizzie asks, "What were some of Michel's clients like? You said yourself you introduced him to some Russians, no? Does anyone know anything about them?"

Sergei seems to consider the question, just looking at her.

"Was he mixed up with some rough types?" she asks.

He nods his head.

"What were they like?"

"Not sure he had any idea just how rough they were. *Titushki*—know what that means?"

Lizzie shakes her head, though she can imagine. *Why did Sergei introduce people like this to Michel?* she thinks.

Sergei says, "Gangsters, basically."

"What do you mean? Why did you introduce him? How do you know people like that?"

"Well, they seem respectable enough: wealthy, well dressed, and often even well educated, or certainly smart. Business acquaintances. In Russia, organized crime has long been part of the banks—indeed, the government—since the time of the czars. After the fall of the Soviet Union the gangsters were really the only ones who knew who they were, what they wanted, and how to get it."

"What do you mean? Why?"

He sighs. "It was such a confusing time for most people. No one knew what to think. Lots of dirty Russian money flooded out of the country and into Western banks as well as into real estate. Russian organized crime was commingled with Western money. No one refused the Russians' money. The West is just as guilty in my opinion."

"You mean these were mafiosi, Michel's clients, your business partners?" Lizzie asks.

"Some. All sorts of people go into real estate—you'd be surprised—for various reasons."

"What sort of people?" She looks at Sergei, whose gaze shifts, as it does so often, now out the window into the night.

"Russian oligarchs, for example, people with too much money and too few scruples."

"How did you get mixed up with people like that?" she asks anxiously, thinking of the gun in his drawer.

"Because of my background, obviously—the language, and I know both markets. I started out here as a more or less starving teenager, after all. Came to join an uncle who disappeared fast. No fancy university for me. My parents couldn't get visas. You know the story—you can imagine what I was obliged to do to survive. I had to hustle and I did—I learned the ropes, so they come to me for information, help with their businesses."

In the moonlight Lizzie watches his face, which seems without expression as he speaks. *What is he thinking?* she wonders, as she often does when she is with him.

"Dirty businesses? Dirty Russian money? Why do you speak so badly about your own people?" she asks. "I thought you believed Russians were the best, the most gifted, the most talented people in the world."

"Oh, I do," Sergei says, and sighs, leaning back against the sofa. "Talented, even brilliant, very good at what they do—the best in the world. Smart—good chess players in all senses of the word. They know, have always known better than anyone else, the human heart."

"But people who might be dangerous in some way?"

He looks at her and nods. "A mystery, but Russians after Communism have changed."

"Changed in what way?" Lizzie wants to know.

Sergei leans forward, puts his elbows on his knees and his head between his hands. "Paranoid, frightened to speak up, after the *cheka*—the KGB—look what happened to my poor father. People were so used to watching what they said. It required tremendous courage to speak out directly to tell the truth."

"Don't you think people are like that everywhere—frightened, unable to think for themselves?" she asks.

"Maybe, but it's worse in Russia; there's no history of democracy. The musicians, the writers, the painters have tried to establish some kind of freedom but even Pushkin was banished, not to speak of people like Dostoevsky or more recently the poets like Akhmatova. At least under the czarist regime they didn't have our modern means to interfere in people's lives. They didn't have radioactive poisons!"

Lizzie says, "And now today, there is no respect for human life?"

Sergei nods his head. "The system has changed, but not the people. They've just spread a flashy veil over the old one. KGB was dissolved, but its officers are still around. Look at the President—dressed like a mob boss and sounds as if he comes from a gangster film. Look at the strut and the quick wary sideways glances. Politicians acting like gangsters, people sacrificed for the needs of the state, used as trading chips, fodder. Look at poor Litvinenko—radioactive poison in his teapot, an excruciatingly painful death. You know Stalin's famous quip: 'If there is no man there is no problem'?"

Lizzie just stares at Sergei and shudders, thinking of how his poor father, a brilliant doctor, threw himself down stone steps in Stalin's prison. Could Pamela be in serious danger?

Sergei goes on, lowering his voice slightly, as if he is afraid someone might hear in the old house, where the walls are thin and sound carries easily. "Buying an apartment or a house is often simply a way to launder money. I've seen people just come in with millions of dollars in cash and plonk it down on a desk at the moment of a sale—takes your breath away."

"And you introduced people like that to Michel?" Lizzie says indignantly.

He shrugs and explains, "I was just trying to help. He needed clients. Many of his more respectable American or French clients had left the bank, repatriated funds, and paid the penalties, or moved it to London, and given up their American citizenship, but these Russians were looking for safe havens, banks that would take their money, without asking any questions."

"Where did they get so much money?" she asks.

"Much of it was just stolen, after the fall of the Soviet Union—Gazprom, Sibneftegaz, the major gas fields, for example. Big banks like UBS and Julius Baer were refusing foreign money that was suspect in any way, and people were scrambling to hide great sums. They were happy to find a smaller, private bank and an obliging banker who was not too choosy. Any bank."

"So you introduced them to Michel," Lizzie says, looking at Sergei's shadowy face in the moonlight. "You introduced him to real crooks—ruthless crooks?"

"I tried to warn him, and I think he was increasingly worried himself. He must have suspected that he was in trouble." He pauses, looks at her, and adds, "He must have known these people were a law unto themselves."

"Do you think they might have gone after Pamela? A fourteen-year-old!" she says, thinking of her blond-headed niece with her wide cheekbones and her dark eyes. What might men of this sort have done to her niece, Lizzie thinks, holding on to the thick arm of the sofa as if it were a rocking ship. "They are not . . . they couldn't be perverts, could they?"

"No, no, that's not the problem, but if she knew something they wanted to know, I'm afraid they wouldn't have stopped at picking her up, and even . . . discarding her without a qualm."

"Like what? What could she possibly have known?" Lizzie watches Sergei, who rises and walks around the big moonlit room nervously, taking great strides on his long, lithe legs. *Why did he introduce people like this to Michel if they were dangerous?*

Lizzie cannot help thinking. He might have had good intentions. He always seems to have good intentions, whatever he does, but what a careless man, careless with other people's lives.

"Who knows? Lots of reasons, Lizzie—which is why, like you, I'm worried about the kid," Sergei says.

PART X

SWITZERLAND

*Saturday Afternoon
and Night; Sunday*

I

PAMELA

1

She sits on the bed and waits to see what will happen. Her heart is beating hard, and her mouth is dry, when someone knocks on the door. It is the maid again, wearing her dark hair neatly drawn back in a thick glossy bun. She looks so clean and nice, with her round face and round head, and Pamela wonders why a woman like this would do this kind of work. She guesses it must be for money. The maid smiles at her, tells her to follow, and ushers her down the green carpeted stairs. She opens a door in the hall and nods to Pamela to enter. Pamela stands in the doorway, looking into a paneled study with book-lined walls and a desk in a bay window, which appears to open on the twilit garden behind.

An older, gray-haired man, not the one who drove her here, sits behind a grand desk with curved legs and a green lamp. He tells her to come in and sit down. "Don't be alarmed," he says in accented English, smiling a phony smile and speaking with phony sympathy. She sits down in the chair that the man indicates opposite the desk. He goes on smiling at her, the sort of smile you use with children when you want to please. She does not smile back. "We just need to ask you a few questions and then we will get you back to school."

She looks at him for a moment before lowering her gaze. She wonders how he can imagine she would be so stupid as to believe him. Why do adults think children are so dumb? He must have no idea of what is in her mind. Now she has seen his face, his villa; he must know she could go and report him to the police, though it is true she is not sure where or who he is. All she knows is he is lying. She feels her growing panic increased by his stupid words.

It is obvious to her that the only way she will be able to leave this place is if she can escape on her own. Furtively she looks around the room for some way out. She stares at the windows behind the man, which seem to open onto a terrace with a railing. She wonders if they are locked and if she could climb over the railing into the garden.

Then she surveys the desk to see if there is any heavy instrument within reach—a stone paperweight she could throw at him, or even a sharp letter opener she could use against the man, though he looks strong. There seems to be nothing but a stack of paper piled on his desk and a gray telephone. Could she kill someone even if she had the strength and a weapon? Could she drive a knife into this man's chest? she wonders. Or slice it across his neck? What is the best place to aim for to kill someone? *Why didn't they teach me that in science class?* she thinks. She has difficulty imagining herself with a knife lifted to plunge into the man's chest.

"Do you like your school?" he asks.

She nods her head.

"Such a good school!" he says with his smooth, oily voice.

She just looks at him and thinks she would probably recognize this man's distinctive voice, his heavy Russian accent, even if she could not remember his face with its plump lips and heavy nose. She understands that he will ask her about her father. She remembers her father saying once that it is easier to tell the truth, as one might easily forget a lie. But her last memory of him, the last thing he did when she asked who was going sailing with him, was put his finger to his lips, the way he would do occasionally if there was something to hide.

The man behind the desk, as she expected, asks her the same question that her father's client asked her in the garden: Does she know the name of the person who was going sailing with her father that morning, or anything about him? They are trying to locate the man's money, which they believe her father invested for him. She shakes her head and says what she said before, telling as much truth as possible, keeping her gaze down, that it was very early in the morning and that she asked to go with her father, but he refused.

The man asks, "There was no mention at any time of a bank account, the name or the number of a bank account? Would you know where your father would keep information of this kind? Apparently there was a notebook which he used habitually—a small blue agenda which has not been found. Would you know where that is?"

She shakes her head, but her heart tilts at the thought that this man knows where this information is kept. She wonders where the blue book is now. She does remember the name of the account: Speranski, an odd name that her father put down in his book beside the number. She hopes her eyes have not given her away as she felt they did in the garden of her own house.

The man says if she could help them find this number and name or the whereabouts of the book, or suggest anywhere else her father might have stored such information that would enable them to access the money, it would be very important to them and to her.

"Would he have kept this information on a computer?"

"He wasn't very good with computers," she admits.

She looks at him and says quite truthfully that there was no mention of money, that her father rarely carried money, or spoke of it. "My father said it was not good manners to mention money. *On ne parle pas de l'argent.*"

The man chuckles at her answer and gives her a surprised grin. "Surely an odd thing for a banker to say! I can't help thinking that you would have known where your father kept this information. Are you certain you do not know where the agenda is kept? Or perhaps even the name and the number of the account? There is a lot of money in this account."

She tells him she has no idea where it is or what is in it.

He looks at her for a moment, and then says, "Because you are such a bright girl I will explain why this information is so important to us. We have power of attorney and just need the number and name of the account to access the money which is ours. Do you understand?"

Pamela sighs and says she wishes she could help him but she cannot.

He looks at her and tells her he is sorry to have had to bring her here under these circumstances; she is obviously an unusually smart young girl, and he knows she was very close to her father. "Such a nice man, your father," he says in his phony voice, looking down at the piece of paper before him, where he has scratched a few lines. "Everyone liked him," he adds in that annoying tone that certain grown-ups use with children as though they were idiots. He adds that she must understand that it is a great deal of money involved and that it belongs legitimately to them and should not be left to molder in a Swiss bank.

Perhaps she will think over his questions and with time the answers may become clear to her, he says, looking at her directly now, his gray-green eyes glimmering, hard as pebbles in a stream, she thinks. He has heard that she has such a good memory. If they do come to her and she is willing to share them, they will let her go immediately. It would be to everyone's advantage. He has no wish to harm her in any way—he loves children—or keep her here longer than necessary. It is all up to her.

She looks back at him and thinks what he calls her good memory has caused her only trouble so far. He says she may go, but he hopes she will consider the matter seriously and realize how important it is to her safety.

2

The maid is waiting in the hall as Pamela walks out of the man's study. She smiles at Pamela in her pleasant way and accompanies her back up the stairs to her room, walking slightly behind her. Pamela notices a fat butler in a gold-and-black-striped uniform who is polishing a round table under a window as they go by.

When the maid has closed the door behind her, Pamela stands close by it and listens as the maid locks it. She hears the key turning twice in the lock. She listens to the conversation in the corridor. The maid is talking to the butler she saw by the window. "Do you think they will kill her?" she asks in Italian.

Pamela cannot hear the man's response, but she hears the maid say, "*Poverina, così giovane,*" which she knows means "Poor thing, so young."

For a moment the room swings around her, and she has to clutch the end of the bed. They can't kill her, Pamela thinks. She must do something. She tries the window again and then the door and then sits down on the bed, banging her heels against the bedspread. She looks around the room for some sort of weapon, but even if she were able to overpower the nice maid, she is certain the front door must be locked, and she senses there are other people in the house. She can hear footsteps, doors opening and closing, voices, the sound of cars coming and going. When she looks out the window she sees fancy black cars coming up the driveway.

Her father would have wanted her to make a plan. She thinks of him and what he would say on the boat if the wind picked up suddenly and blew unusually strongly, or something untoward happened—a leak once in the hull, she remembers, which frightened her. "We will make a plan," he would say, as though with a plan there was always a way out of every situation—and with her father there had always been a way. Sometimes he would say, "Hope is not a plan." He was a planner, looking to the future and optimistic about his chances of making them safe. She sits looking at her smooth white childish hands, the bitten fingernails, trying to make a plan. She tries to think of what her father would have told her to do. What plan would enable her to escape? She can think of nothing but locked doors, a house filled with dangerous people looking only, she understands, for money. She knows whatever the man said about her or her father will not alter things an iota if it is more convenient to get rid of her.

How would they kill her? she wonders. Would they suffocate her with a pillow, perhaps? Or throw her down from a height? Or bludgeon her with a club? Or make her drink poison? She walks up and down, sucking her thumb and wishing she had at least her little old stuffed lamb to stroke.

She sits again, feeling increasingly helpless and afraid. She listens to the noises in the house, people coming and going. She has cramps in her stomach and has to use the bathroom. Time seems to pass so slowly, and she cannot think of how to escape.

Finally, she hears the key turn in the door, and the maid comes back into the room. "I brought you something to eat, dear. I thought you might be hungry. They have given you nothing all day," she says in Italian with a hint of reproach in her voice. She is carrying a heaped plate of spaghetti, a fork, a glass, a bottle of Coca-Cola, and a piece of bread on a tray.

Pamela smiles at this kindness, a gift of food, which she understands the maid has taken upon herself to offer. She thanks her, though she has no appetite. She stares at her and remembers how her father would always say, "People like to talk about themselves. You have to find a way to make this possible." She asks the maid in Italian if she has any children. The maid is putting the tray down on the desk and she turns her head and smiles, obviously surprised. She says, "*Come parla bene l'Italiano!* How well you speak Italian! Who taught you?"

Pamela looks at her directly and says, "My father did, but now he is dead, and I am here, locked up in this house of evil," and the tears come to her eyes. The maid comes over to her and puts her hand gently on Pamela's head. She strokes her hair. "*Poverina, così giovane,*" she says again, shaking her head. She tells Pamela she has four children, all naughty boys, and that she would have liked to have a pretty young girl just like her.

Pamela smiles up at her and says, "Girls are best!"

When the maid turns to leave the room, Pamela follows her, puts her hand on her arm, and whispers to her, "Please! Leave the door open." The woman looks at her for a moment, considering, Pamela can see. She repeats "Please!" and puts her hands together in a position of prayer, widening her eyes. She says, "You could save my life." She can see that the maid's eyes are filled with sympathy but at the same time wary. "My mother's heart would be broken if they killed me," she adds. Then the woman turns and leaves. Pamela stands at the door and listens. She hears the sound of the key turning in the lock.

3

Pamela lies fully dressed on the bed, listening to the sounds in the house. She is not sure how many people are here, or where they are all sleeping. Whatever these people are doing, it goes on for what feels to her like a long time.

She determines she must wait, however long it takes, until all is quiet, and then she must attempt to escape. She has a plan in mind.

She thinks of her "circus," the little animals she collected as a child and took to bed with her—the lion, the giraffe, the little pink pig—believing they protected her, kept her safe in the dark. She wishes she had them here with her, though she no longer believes they are alive, as she did as a small child, when she thought everything—not just rivers and trees and the sky, but all sorts of objects, like chairs and tables and knives—was alive.

She remembers her father's stories about Algeria, the land of his early childhood, a land that he loved, the vast spaces, the hills, the sea, a small white horse. She imagines his shock upon finding his own father hanging by his necktie, dead in the bathroom, something he told her about only recently.

She is afraid the maid might come back to reclaim the plate of food, which Pamela cannot eat in her anxiety, though she has had a sip of Coke. Or someone might come in the room to see if she is sleeping.

She waits until very late, when the house is completely silent. She can hear nothing, and she is afraid she, too, will fall asleep and miss the opportunity to try and escape if she does not get up now.

Finally, she takes off her shoes, turns out her bedside light, and waits for her eyes to adjust to the darkness. Then she goes into the bathroom, looking at the small window over the toilet. She is not sure if she can fit through the space but she will try. She climbs up onto the top of the toilet in her socks, and struggles to open the window. To her relief it opens onto the night air. She puts both hands on the edge of the window and with an effort manages to lift herself up. She drags herself through the small opening so that she can look down at the ground below, trying to calculate the distance. She gets back down, takes her shoes and throws them down, and listens to them land. In the half dark and with the light of the moon she thinks she could let herself down with her sheets if she could knot them together and tie them securely to the handle of the window.

She goes back into the bedroom, quickly strips her bed, and ties the two sheets together with a sheet bend, a knot that her father taught her on the boat. Then she pushes the sheets through the window and lets them drop down, looping them several times around the window handle as securely as she can. She can see they don't reach the ground but dangle there in the air, white and visible to anyone who might pass by. Can she jump that far? She must hurry before someone sees the white sheets.

She has difficulty pulling herself completely through the small opening of the window. Fortunately she is slender and has recently lost weight since her father died, but she struggles to get her broad shoulders through into the night, then hangs on to the ledge until the last moment, afraid to try the sheets and slither to the ground. She manages to let herself down, hand over hand, so afraid the sheets will give way or someone will see her descending. She hangs for a moment in the air, hesitating before she forces herself to take the plunge into nothingness. She lets herself drop into the void, landing with a dull thud, which sounds so loud to her, the ground hard beneath the soles of her feet, the shock like knives up her shins.

Trembling all over, she feels the cool night air on her whole body with relief. She stands shaking in the half light, leaning against the wall of the house, looking around, hoping no one will notice the sheets. The moon lights up the trees, the ground, and the sky is clear. She gathers up her shoes and hurriedly makes her way down some stone steps, which seem to lead into what she senses is the garden; she can smell the fresh pine needles, feel them prickling under her socks, and she hears night birds and crickets. Quietly she puts on her shoes and goes as fast as she can, through the bushes and trees, feeling her way, moving toward what she hopes is the road. She can see Orion low in the sky, and she follows the sounds she can hear of a few cars in the distance. She hears a rustling in the leaves and branches and stands leaning against a tree for a moment, fearing someone is following her.

She wishes she'd had her phone on her when the man came to her in the garden at school. Now she stumbles on in the half dark, tripping over branches and roots, afraid she will fall, or that someone has seen the sheets and will come running after her and catch up with her. Eventually, to her relief, she comes to the road.

Terrified someone might be following her and might see her

in the light of the oncoming cars, she runs along the edge in the bushes until she can run no farther. Then she crouches, trembling, in the shadows at the edge of the road. She asks her father for the strength to go on, to find her way. *Please help me!* she prays. She is exhausted and beginning to feel helpless and so lonely in the dark.

She starts walking backward along the road, lifting her thumb the way she has seen people do. At first she is so glad to have left the villa, to have managed to find her way to the road, and she finds the moonlight shining on the road beautiful; the lights of each coming car seem a promise of escape. But there are not many cars at this late hour, and those that come pass her by fast, without stopping, going on into the night. Why don't they stop? The cars continue to pass her, lighting up the road for only a brief moment of hope as she goes on walking backward through the night.

Eventually, a truck comes shuddering to a stop, and she clambers up on the step on the driver's side to ask him if she can go with him. She can see his dark, unshaven face and his small slanting eyes dimly in the half light as he looks at her askance. What, she wonders then, if he is one of the Russians from the big villa and has come out to find her?

She wonders, too, if this is wise, if it is safe to go with this stranger who stares at her so disapprovingly. She remembers the lecture at school about the dangers of talking to strange men. "Never take a lift from someone you don't know," the teacher warned. Should she run on alone? But how far can she get on foot? Staring at her, he asks in French, "What on earth are you doing out in the night alone? Where do you think you are going?"

She considers what she should say, her mouth dry with fear. She contemplates telling the truth, saying something dramatic to impress the man, evoke his pity, to tell him that she is running away from danger, that it is a question of life and death, or asking him if he can take her back to her school. She remembers her father saying, "Never trust anyone completely," and decides it might be wiser to ask the man simply if she can ride along with him for a while. Above all she needs to get away from the villa and the people in it, and it does not really matter where he is going.

The man looks at her and says, "Running away from home, so young? Are you sure that's something you want to do? Is this wise?"

She nods her head speechlessly, tears coming into her eyes.

He sighs and says, "Well, I'm not going very far, just to make a delivery of some fruit at a hotel in Lugano. If you like you can come with me."

"That would be perfect," she says, thinking she should probably not go back to her school in any case, for a while. The Russians will be looking for her.

Before the man can change his mind, she goes around the truck and struggles with the door, which he leans across to open for her. She hops in. In the light of the cab, she can see that the man driving the truck has a round face and a potbelly, or it seems so to her in the half light. He shrugs and tells her to buckle up. He says he is willing to take her with him as far as he is going. He speaks in a sort of whisper, as though the words are caught in his throat, and the truck smells of cigarette smoke, but to her relief he takes off, going excruciatingly slowly down the road.

She wants to ask him to step on the accelerator but instead asks, "How far is it?"

"Shouldn't be too far now," he says. "A couple of hours. Doze if you like. Get some beauty sleep."

She realizes instinctively that it would be impolite and perhaps dangerous. The man does not look dangerous, but she remembers her father once saying that those people who are polite and seem charming are often the most dangerous. She is not going to sleep but will watch the man's face, his hands. She must be ready to jump out of the cab if she has to, she thinks.

Though she has never done this before, she devises that the work of a hitchhiker, surely, particularly one without any money on her, is to amuse the driver. So she asks him some polite questions the way her father taught her to, about his family, his work, his interests. He smiles at her and seems glad of the company in the lonely night. They drive on for what feels like a long time in the dark. It seems like a hundred years since she sat in the school garden after breakfast on Saturday morning and the man came to her. Yet, she reminds herself, it is only a day and a night. She feels her head falling forward onto her chest but struggles to remain awake, wary of danger, looking at the man beside her as well as behind them from time to time to see if anyone is following them or if anyone is aware she has escaped yet. As far as she can tell there is no one hovering behind them. She scans the few signposts she can see in the headlights of the truck, but does not recognize the names.

When they finally come into the town and drive slowly through the almost empty streets, she has difficulty keeping her eyes open.

She feels she has been traveling forever without any sleep. They go up a long driveway as the day is breaking, the sky striped with pink, the trees black above them. She sees the sun rising over the lake behind the hotel—a fancy hotel. She wonders what she should do now. Will they even let her walk into a place of this kind? Will they stop her at the top of the marble steps that lead under an awning into the hotel with its bougainvillea creepers? Perhaps no one will notice her at this early hour, she hopes, smoothing her crumpled skirt.

The trucker stops his vehicle in the parking lot near a service entrance in the early morning light. He turns to her and asks her what she is going to do now and how she will manage. She smiles and shrugs and says she will be all right, though she realizes how reluctant she is to leave the relative security of his truck. She wants to ask him if he could take her home with him.

He looks at her closely, as if he can imagine what she is thinking. He asks if she has any money, anyone she can call. She shakes her head. He takes out a wad of folded Swiss francs from his pocket and peels off a few, which he gives her. "Call your family, is my advice. Go home, girl," he says. "I don't know what you are running away from or why, but you are much too young to be out on your own. It is a dangerous world out there," he warns her.

"Thank you for your kindness," she says. She thinks he is surely right. These people who have carried her off would not hesitate to get rid of her, now that they know she could endanger them.

"Thank you for the pleasant company," he says with a smile, and wishes her good luck as she gets out of the truck. She makes an effort to walk with elegance: her head held high, placing one foot in front of the other, not looking left or right, her legs stiff, her shins sore from her drop to the ground. She goes up the steps under the pink awning in her borrowed navy skirt. She prays no one will stop her. She is exhausted and famished. She has had no sleep and no food for a day and a night. At the top of the steps she turns and waves her fingers at the trucker, who honks his horn encouragingly, a blast that makes her shudder.

II

ALICE

1

Alice cannot sleep after talking to the headmaster, though it is still night for her. She tries to lie quietly on the double bed in the small hotel room but tosses and turns despite the thick, drawn curtains. She senses the sun rising outside her window, time passing without her daughter, her terror catching her at the throat. She must do something.

She considers calling Lizzie, but Lizzie will be with Sergei and Alice does not want to disturb them in the night.

Finally she cannot wait any longer and decides to call her little sister, even if it means waking her and perhaps Sergei. Lizzie will surely see the situation more clearly and will tell her frankly what she thinks Alice should do. So she calls her and listens to her sleepy voice saying, "Hello? Hello? Alice? Where are you?"

"In a hotel room in Zurich," Alice says, and apologizes for leaving the house so abruptly without even saying good-bye and waking her now at one in the morning. She tells Lizzie about her call to the headmaster, and how awful the man was.

"What did he say?" Lizzie asks after a pause.

Alice says she cannot believe the school is so callous and cavalier about the whole matter. "How could they not have notified the police immediately? How could the teachers and even Pamela's friends imagine this was some sort of fugue on her part? Children, particularly those in a state of grief, are known to run away from school, the school psychologist had said, apparently," she says.

"Bullshit!" Lizzie says in her direct way. She says it is clear the school prefers to see this as a rash act on the part of one of their students, to blame Pamela rather than to imagine something that might make them liable for negligence.

"They seem to have just let her wander around in that big garden on her own. So bad for her! No one knew where she went after breakfast! All they want is to hush things up, to preserve the school's reputation, which I'm beginning to think is completely undeserved. They just want to make it look as if Pamela bolted out of the blue," Alice says, getting angrier and more worried as she speaks. "I don't believe for a minute she would have behaved so irrationally."

"Why would she have run away if school was where she wanted to be?" Lizzie says, making Alice even more worried than she was before.

"She might have changed her mind—perhaps things didn't pan out as she expected, but surely she would have called me then!"

Lizzie says, "I've been talking to Sergei and he seems worried that some of his Russian colleagues might be involved in some way in all of this. He says some of Michel's clients were not entirely to be trusted."

"What do you mean? How could Michel's clients be involved? Did Sergei give you any names, any way to find these people?" Alice asks, but Lizzie answers vaguely, without any real information. Finally Alice says she will keep Lizzie informed if she has any news and puts down her phone. She has talked herself into such a state of worry and despair that she takes a sleeping pill and sleeps heavily.

When the phone rings Alice is fast asleep. She is dreaming that Pamela is sleeping safely beside her. They are in Beaulieu-sur-Mer, and Pamela has climbed up into her bed as she sometimes would do as a small child. She can smell her sweet soapy smell, feel her thick hair on her cheek.

For a moment in the dark, with the heavy curtains drawn, hearing her phone ring, Alice thinks it must be the headmaster calling back with some news of Pamela. In the early morning, half-awake, she is filled with remorse and regret. Why did she let her child go back to school? The headmaster must surely have spoken to the police, and they have helped in some way. She fumbles around desperately on the bedside table to find her cell phone. She turns on the light and then picks it up. It is not the headmaster's voice.

Despite her befuddled state of mind, waking from a deep sleep, Alice recognizes the beloved voice on the telephone. Pamela speaks softly, her voice trembling. "Mommy? Is that you?"

Alice exclaims, "Pamela! Darling! Where on earth are you? Are you all right?"

"Can you come and get me? You must make sure no one

follows you. They might follow you. You must be very careful," Pamela says in a faint dull voice.

"Of course I will come immediately, darling. Where are you? Just tell me. I'm so happy to hear your voice. I was so worried. Who would want to follow me? No one knows where I am."

"Where are you?" Pamela asks.

"In a hotel in Zurich. I arrived from New York early this morning. I was planning on going to your school today to see if I could get some information about you. Spoke to them earlier and told them to notify the police."

There is a moment's silence, and Alice is terrified the connection has broken. Where is the child? What is she talking about? Then Pamela says, "You must promise not to tell anyone where you are going. Don't trust anyone. It's very important no one knows or follows you. You might lead them to me. Someone might be watching. Come as quickly as you can. Bring some money. I will be waiting for you in the lounge or if they turn me out in the garden of the hotel—"

"Which hotel, where? Where are you, darling?" Alice asks desperately.

"Hotel Labelle in Lugano. A fancy hotel on the lake. I have to go. I managed to find someone who would lend me her phone but I have to get off. Be careful," she says, and before Alice can say anything else, Pamela has hung up.

Alice looks up the hotel on her phone immediately. Her hands tremble so she can hardly type in the address, making mistakes as she looks for directions to the hotel. She is not even quite sure where Lugano is. All she knows is that she must get to the love of her life as soon as she can. Pamela sounded completely stunned to her. Why would anyone be following her? Has she lost her mind? Or is she in serious danger of some kind? Whatever it is, Alice has only one desire, and that is to be with her, to hold her safely in her arms.

She must go immediately. Still, she decides to leave the place quietly, making sure she is not seen. They have her American Express card number, after all, and they can charge her for her night in the room. She will have to rent a car, though, which seems the quickest way to Lugano and the Hotel Labelle, as far as she can tell, but she decides to tell them at her hotel that she is going to Geneva and will be back.

She dresses quickly, fumbling with her clothes, catching her hair in the dress zip, thrusting her feet fast into her flat shoes. Hastily she slings her belongings into her leather backpack. She has brought almost nothing with her. She sends a brief text to Lizzie—"Gone to help Pamela. Will send news soon."—and goes down to rent the car.

2

The concierge is happy to arrange a car rental, though everything seems to take much longer than it should, and the necessary actions seem increasingly absurd: filling out forms, finding her driving license, her credit card. She fumbles through her backpack, desperately afraid she has lost the necessary documents and her passport and will never be able to get to her daughter.

She drives all through what is left of the morning without

stopping, getting lost in her state of confusion and anxiety in her rented car. Despite Google Maps, she manages to take several wrong turns. It is early afternoon, local time, when to her relief she finally finds herself in Lugano and at the hotel. She leaves the keys in the car, lets a hotel valet park it for her, and walks quickly up the steps and under the pink awning, into the large hotel lounge. She strides through the big quiet reception rooms of the four-star hotel, looking around at the pink silk sofas and Louis Quinze chairs, the pink silk framing the windows, which look over the lake. This orderly, quiet, static world seems strangely removed from her, as though she is looking at it dimly from a distance and through pebbled glass. None of it seems quite real to her. How can this be happening—an ordinary Sunday afternoon in September in Switzerland? Nothing that she sees reflects her panic, her trembling body, her fast-beating heart, her lost darling, her loss and her longing for Michel. How can life continue so calmly, with people smiling and even laughing contentedly around her?

There are few people here, mostly gray-haired and elderly, sitting at tables calmly drinking coffee or tea or already having drinks, nibbling nuts, and talking quietly, their heads close, ice chinking in their glasses. With something like envy she watches a youngish couple with a small boy and girl who are eating ice cream.

But *where* is her Pamela? Where is *her* darling girl? What could have happened to her? Has Alice come to the right place? Did she misunderstand the child's address? she wonders. Or is there perhaps another Hotel Labelle in Lugano? She fears the hotel personnel in such a fancy place might have turned her daughter out—or might she be hiding somewhere near? Surely someone could not have come and picked her up. She glances at her watch.

She walks out onto the terrace and gazes across the sparkling water, which makes her shiver. She thinks of Michel and his strange gray distorted face, the grimace of . . . was it disgust? Had his last thoughts been of her, his disappointment and lack of faith in her truthfulness, her honesty?

She surveys the smooth lawn that runs down to the lake, the weeping willows, the neat border of early autumn flowers. Such a beautiful place, she thinks.

Alice is moving toward the reception area, about to ask the prim-looking concierge if he has seen a young girl in the lounge, when the pink curtain with its yellow birds of paradise lifts gently in the breeze from the lake and then is drawn back, like a flag, as though, she feels, beckoning to her. She walks over and looks behind the Louis Quinze sofa and sees a blond head, the dusty schoolgirl shoes. Someone lies sleeping there, on her side. To her infinite relief, she realizes it is Pamela, curled up into a ball on the floor.

She crouches down quietly and puts her hand on her daughter's head, strokes her hair. She says softly, "Pamela, darling," and Pamela wakes and looks up at her mother and smiles. Her face is pale, with dark shadows under her big eyes. Alice helps her up.

"Mommy! I thought I was dreaming! You came! You came!"

"Of course I came! Of course I came," Alice says, holding Pamela close in her arms. She wants to hold on to her slight trembling body forever, never to let her daughter go. How could she have allowed her to go off on her own back to boarding school? How could she have ever let her out of her sight? Pamela weeps and heaves hysterically in her arms, and Alice guides her gently to the sofa, where they can sit side by side, holding on to each other. Alice wishes they were on the old sofa in the house in Amagansett, safe with her sister.

Pamela says, "I was so scared. So scared. I thought they would kill me. I didn't sleep all last night."

Alice says, "It's all right now. It's all going to be all right now, darling." Then, when she has wiped Pamela's eyes and kissed her on both her plump cheeks repeatedly, and Pamela has quieted down sufficiently, realizing that the people in the lounge are all staring at them, Alice says, "I'm going to see if we can get a room here, darling, all right?" And she walks over to the man at the reception desk and asks if they have a room available for a night.

He looks her up and down. She is still in her crumpled clothes. Her hair is disheveled, she knows. She smooths it back with her hand.

The man shifts his gaze from Alice to Pamela, who has followed her and is hovering behind her mother in her creased, dusty navy skirt. Where on earth did the child get that awful skirt? The man sniffs suspiciously and says he will see what he can do, that the hotel is very full.

Alice takes her platinum American Express card out of her wallet and her passport and slaps them down on the marble counter. She says she is naturally willing to pay in advance for one of their best rooms on the lake. The man straightens up slightly and looks more enthusiastic, raises his thick eyebrows, and sighs. He eventually comes up with an old-fashioned, heavy wooden key. As he hands it over to her he smiles and says, "I'm glad someone came for the young girl. We have been keeping an eye on her. We were worried."

Alice puts her arm around Pamela and squeezes her tight to her side. "How long have you been here?" she asks.

"It feels like forever. I had to find someone who would lend me a phone, and then I called you and waited. I was so afraid you wouldn't find me or someone else would!" Pamela says, as they take the old paneled elevator up to the fifth floor.

Inside the big hotel room with its twin beds and chintz bedspreads, its comfortable armchairs, Alice opens the curtains on the afternoon light and the view of the sparkling lake. She turns to her child, who is locking the door from the inside with the bolt.

"I am so glad you are safe. I was so, so worried!" she says, wrapping the child in her arms.

Pamela relaxes into her mother's embrace again and says, "I thought I was going to die. This man came to the school with a gun and made me go in his car and took me for miles and miles with a horrid black thing over my face."

"Who are these people?" Alice asks. "Who would do this to you?"

Pamela looks at her mother and asks if they can eat something before she explains. She says she has had only two cups of coffee and a brioche since she arrived here. She only had the few Swiss francs from the trucker who had picked her up, and she was so afraid they would turn her out of the lounge. She sat there using the toilet, drinking water from the tap, and hoping they would let her stay all day. The coffees were the cheapest things on the menu. Finally she hid behind the sofa, so afraid they might make her leave, but when she lay down, she fell asleep. Alice can only wipe the child's tears and hold her. She says she's starving, too; she hasn't been able to eat or sleep since she heard Pamela was missing on Saturday morning. She picks up the phone and orders room service, Pamela's favorite food: steak.

3

As they eat side by side at the table in the hotel room in the afternoon sunshine, Alice tries to get Pamela to explain what happened.

"Some Russian people—their accent sounded Russian—are looking for a man who was with Daddy," Pamela says. "They want the number and name of his account at the bank."

"You mean, someone who was supposed to meet Daddy on his boat?" Alice asks.

Pamela nods. "I think the Russian must have given Daddy a lot of money to keep in the bank and these people want it."

"And that's why they want to know where he is?"

Nodding again, Pamela says, "I think they're looking for the man because they want the money. He must have been one of Daddy's clients."

"I see," Alice says, though nothing is very clear to her. She looks at her daughter's pale face and bright gaze, her big mouth, which she is filling with grilled steak, and wants to give her another kiss on both her wide cheeks. Has Pamela understood all

of this correctly? she wonders. At fourteen years old she has always seemed so grown-up and smart to Alice, who remembers
being such an innocent at that age. She knew nothing about the
real world, certainly nothing about money or banks, secret accounts, secret numbers, even after her mother died and she was
obliged to step into her shoes.

"So why did these people come for you, darling? How could
you possibly help them?" Alice asks.

"They thought I might know where the information was kept.
They know Daddy and I were close and that I often traveled with
him. They thought he might have told me where he keeps his
records of the secret money that would help them to find it."

Alice can easily imagine these people, whoever they are, might
come to this conclusion. Pamela has always seemed like a savvy
child, she thinks, spending so much of her time traveling with
her father, going to fancy hotels in the world's big cities, wandering through the streets and visiting museums in European
capitals, which she loved to do. What really happened on those
voyages? Alice speculates now, looking at her daughter, who
looks so pale, her blond hair falling in her face, tears coming to
her eyes so easily. Was she wrong to let her go off alone with her
father on his business trips? *Were they as innocent as I imagined?*
she thinks, her heart beating hard.

"Did you know anything to tell these people? Where did they
take you?" Alice wonders what sort of people Michel was mixed
up with and why. What purpose did the child serve on these
voyages? Was it just love that made Michel want to take her
along?

Alice, when she thinks about it, always imagined Michel's clients as stout elderly dowagers out of Henry James who needed someone kind and obliging to sort out their finances for them, or very rich young foreigners who did not know what to do with their fortunes and wanted someone honest and discreet and safe. She knew some of these people were probably evading taxes, but she did not blame them terribly, thinking of what certain governments did with their money: the unjust wars that were fought, the corruption clogging the wheels of government in so many places. She knew Michel was always honest in his dealings and scrupulous in the interests of his clients.

She realizes now how convenient it was for her to think so. She took advantage of the time on her own to work on her music, to advance her own career, to have the joy of playing her violin for hours, of perfecting her art, but now look what has happened. How could she have been so selfish, so willfully blind?

Pamela says, "These were very bad people, Mommy. The maid said they might kill me. I think Daddy must have put this man's money in a secret account, and it was probably illegal money that he was keeping in the bank for him, and these people want access to his account."

"And no one knows where this Russian is?"

"He seems to have disappeared, too, and they want to find him, or rather his money. That's what they are looking for, I think," Pamela says softly in her serious way.

"And do you know where your father would have kept this sort of information, darling?" Alice asks, watching Pamela sitting beside her, eating with great gusto, grease around her mouth.

"I do know the name and the number of the account. Daddy

put it down in his blue agenda he kept in the secret drawer in his desk. I looked at the number and memorized it. What happened to the blue agenda?"

"I have no idea," Alice says, sipping her coffee. "I sold most of the furniture, but we cleaned everything out before it was sold, of course."

Pamela looks at her mother with her big dark sorrowful eyes. So many things sold, so many things gone, Alice thinks. Thank God her daughter is here safe with her.

Alice says, "I wonder how we might find this person. If your father was with him on the boat then he might know what happened to him." This man must know something about Michel's death. She wonders if she should simply go to the police at this point, if it might actually be the best thing to do. "Do you think we should call the police, Pamela? And give them the name of the account and the number? Tell them what has happened? They would hunt for him for us. Wouldn't that be safer for you and for me? What do you think?"

"I don't think Daddy would have liked that. He didn't like the police, the authorities, and this was all a secret—secret account, secret money, a secret client, a secret name which I'm never supposed to talk about," Pamela says seriously, looking at her mother with her big dark eyes. "Daddy said silence was the most important thing."

Alice stares at her daughter and thinks that Michel is now dead, silenced forever, and surely none of this could matter to him. This Russian is probably some kind of crook, engaged in money laundering, who has perhaps gone off with someone else's money. Who knows what might have happened on the boat with this man and Michel, but she doesn't like to say that to the child who adored her father and believed he could do no wrong. In Pamela's eyes, Alice understands, her father was a sort of Robin Hood, taking from the rich to give to the poor, rather than the other way around, or at least a James Bond keeping state secrets for the good of the world.

Alice wonders if Michel knew something might happen to him the morning he left. Why had he doubled his life insurance at that point? Did it have nothing to do with her, with Michel's discovery of the letter she had received from Luigi? Was she, then, in no way responsible for this death?

It seems to Alice that the only person who could answer all these questions is this Russian, dangerous though he may be. She would like to find this man who might be able to tell her more about Michel's death. What did happen on the boat? she wonders. Was it an accident? What about the blow to the head? Would this man tell her? What if he were responsible for a crime?

Then she thinks of the school and the headmaster, who has probably let the police know by now Pamela is missing. She must surely inform them that Pamela has been found.

"The first thing we should do is let your school know you are safe. They must all be so worried about you: your friends and your teachers, the headmaster, after all. Let's just give them a ring. I won't tell them where we are if you are frightened about that, and who knows—you might be right. These people might follow us here, though if the police have been involved now I don't think they could."

There is also the possibility of calling the police directly, Alice thinks, and getting them to look for the Russian, but Pamela does not seem to want her to do that. Nor does Alice know how helpful that would be. Pamela does not know the name of these Russian people, or even if they are really Russians, and apparently she has hardly seen them. One of them was wearing a hat and dark glasses, she said, and she could hardly see his face. Nor does she have a precise idea of where the villa is located. "You say the villa is about two and a half hours from Lugano?"

"I think so, but it might be nearer," Pamela says. "Time seemed so long in the truck. I was so nervous with the strange man. I wasn't even wearing a watch, and I didn't have my cell phone, and it was night so I couldn't see much. I was so tired and frightened. The trucker spoke French and I tried to read the signposts but I couldn't really think straight. I know it was somewhere in the mountains."

"Let's call the school anyway, and just speak to someone briefly. Okay? Do you want to talk to one of your teachers? And they can let the police know you have been found. Then we can decide what to do."

Pamela nods her head, but once she has the phone in her hands and her teacher's voice on the other end all she can do is weep. Alice quickly takes the phone and explains Pamela is safe, just tired out and a little upset and badly frightened. They just wanted to let the school and the police know. Alice says it might be better to give them a few days to rest up and then they will give the school and the police more information if necessary. "We are just going to stay where we are. It's safer for Pamela, or that's what she feels," Alice says firmly, and hopes it is indeed possible. She asks them to send Pamela's belongings as quickly as possible to a PO box in Lugano. They need, above all, her passport.

Pamela's teacher seems all too happy to agree with anything Alice suggests. It is clear she wants to hang up the phone without asking too closely about her favorite pupil's welfare or where she has been or even why. She promises to call the police immediately and clear up the matter, and to make sure that Pamela's belongings are safely and expediently sent.

Alice determines she must find this Russian who may have been with Michel, whatever it may cost. It is the only way to regain her peace of mind, to know if she was responsible in any way for his death.

4

When they have finished their meal, Pamela walks around the big room, peeps into the vast black-and-white-tiled bathroom, and looks behind the shower curtain that covers the bathtub. She says, "What a lovely big tub!" and asks if she could take a bath. They don't have baths at school, only showers, and she loves bathing. She feels cold, and a bath would warm her up. Alice says she thinks that would be an excellent idea. She runs a hot bath and helps Pamela to undress as though she were a little girl once again. The sight of the girl's slight shivering body, her trembling hands, her flushed cheeks move Alice almost to tears. How could this have happened to her daughter? How much of this was her own fault? What sort of a mother has she been? She speculates whether this is all the fruit of her own obsession with her career. Why has she been running after the elusive quicksilver of fame, leaving her child alone? She remembers Pamela as a small child and how she loved to play for hours in the bath, splashing about with her plastic animals, how early she learned to swim in the pool in Amagansett, and then how she would go off sailing so enthusiastically with her father in Beaulieu-sur-Mer.

It is now clear to her that Pamela is in a state of shock. She lies in the hot water weeping softly, while Alice sits in the steamy room beside her on a stool. She sings one of the old lullabies she would sing to her when she was very little, a lullaby Alice's mother would sing to both of her two girls.

Pamela says between sobs that she feels so ashamed. Why did she not go to America, where she would have been safe with her mother? "I should have gone with you!" she wails.

"I should never have let you go. It was Djamilla who persuaded me, actually. She seemed to think you would be happier in your school."

"What if the Russians have traced me to this hotel? What will we do?" Pamela asks her mother.

"Little chance of that, darling," Alice says, hoping it is true. "They could hardly come storming in here. It would be easy for us to call the police. I'm here now and I promise I'll stay right by your side. No one is going to hurt you," she says, but she thinks it will be necessary to get to the bottom of all of this. She needs to know who this man is who was with Michel the day he died, and what happened on the boat.

She washes Pamela's back for her with a sponge, and then the child, as if she could read her mind or perhaps has the same questions in hers, says, "You know who might be able to help us with this?"

"Who?" Alice asks.

"Djamilla."

Alice looks at her daughter and asks, "How could she help?" though she thinks of how helpful Djamilla was after Michel's death. She remembers her bringing in her delicious breakfast in the mornings, opening up the curtains and letting the bright sunlight into her room.

Pamela says, "She always seemed to know everything, and she loved Daddy so much. Daddy told her lots of things. Perhaps more than he even told us. He trusted her completely. Perhaps she has the blue agenda."

"Do you happen to remember her telephone number?"

Pamela says she knows it by heart, and Alice suggests they try and call her. "That's a good plan," Pamela says, brightening visibly. "I bet she'll know. Daddy probably told her about this man, too. They were always whispering together about different people, about you and about me, too. Let's talk to her."

Alice looks at her daughter and feels suddenly happy, seeing her face brighten. For the first time since Michel died she feels really happy—happy to be with her darling girl, happy to see her smile, happy that the sinking sun is still shining outside on the water, in the late afternoon, that the bathroom is warm, clean, and comfortable, the old-fashioned bathtub so large, the towels thick and warm, the bath mat soft. She wishes she could freeze the moment with her child, that they could always be together like this, in the bright, clear light. She will find this man and clarify the mystery, without involving Pamela, she thinks.

Alice helps Pamela out of the bath, the water dripping off her young, slender shape. She wraps her in one of the big fluffy white towels that are draped over warming pipes and then into the robe and slippers the hotel provides for its guests.

Alice picks up the pen and the pad from the bedside table, and asks Pamela to write down Djamilla's number and the name of the secret account with its number. Pamela looks at her mother with her big dark eyes, and after a moment of hesitation, as if she does not even trust her own mother with this information, she sits down on the bed and writes the Russian name on the piece of paper for her mother. She says the name aloud: "Speranski."

Alice sits beside her daughter and repeats the name. She has heard this name before, she thinks, as she says softly, "Speranski . . . Speranski . . . Speranski." She says the name until she can say it easily, almost as if it is a magic spell she is murmuring, one that might conjure up a prince.

Then she punches in the number Pamela has written down. A voice answers almost immediately. "*Allo! Allo!*" the woman says quite clearly. Alice speaks to her in French. "*Djamilla, c'est madame, Madame Alice.*"

"*Qui? C'est qui?*" the woman asks.

"*Madame Alice.*"

Djamilla—she recognizes the voice on the line; Alice mouths to Pamela that it is Djamilla—now asks how she is. "*Comment va la petite? Comment va mon petit chou?*" How is the little one? How is my little cabbage? She wants to know.

Alice says they are both fine now, but she needs some information. "How are you? Where are you? Can you talk?" she asks Djamilla.

Djamilla says she is back in Algeria with her family. She is happy to be home, where she can hear the call to prayer in the air. "Why is Pamela not in her school?" she asks.

Alice says, "Pamela is worried because some acquaintances of her father's—she thinks they might be Russians—are looking for the account name and number to access some money which Michel was keeping for a client, a Russian, in a secret account. The account was called Speranski. Do you know anything about this man, this Russian client of Michel's?"

Djamilla says she does remember Michel speaking of this client but she doesn't remember his name or know anything about his account. Alice tells herself she is absurdly clutching at straws. How would Djamilla know this client of Michel's, if that is who he was? Then Djamilla says that she might be able to find the name in Michel's *carnet bleu*, the little blue book where he kept all his secret information, if it is necessary.

"You have Michel's little blue book?" Alice asks, surprised, remembering Michel snapping the elastic back around his old-fashioned blue address book. Why did he give his old nanny his book?

"I do. He told me to take it from his desk. He thought it was safer. Let me look for it and call me back in an hour or so," she says.

5

Alice waits in a state of anxiety, walking up and down the shadowy room. She has drawn the curtains, lit one small lamp, and watches as Pamela curls up in the hotel robe and falls asleep on one of the beds. She is obviously exhausted, and the hot meal and the hot bath have enabled her to relax and now fall fast sleep. Alice covers her with a blanket and sits by her side, just staring at her face and gently stroking her hair, happy to be beside her. She waits for an hour or so before going into the bathroom and shutting the door behind her so that she can call Djamilla back and not wake her daughter. She sits down on a small stool.

This time Djamilla asks her to spell the account name again, and after Alice has spelled it out a few times Djamilla finds it in the book with the account number as well as a cell phone number.

"I remember the man now. I do remember this man. He came to the house once. Don't you remember monsieur talking about him?"

"I suppose I do," Alice says, thinking of Michel stumbling into the room half-drunk and saying something about a Russian client. The memory was wiped from her mind by all the subsequent drama.

"I did not like him, though monsieur did. Better not to have anything to do with him."

Djamilla adds, "Much love to my little Pamela. Please give her much love from me."

"Would you give me the man's number?" Alice asks.

And with obvious reluctance Djamilla recites the cell phone number, which Alice writes down. "*Fais attention*—be careful! *C'est un homme dangereux*! He's a dangerous man. I told monsieur not to have anything to do with him! But he wouldn't listen to me! Such a stubborn man!"

"Why dangerous?" Alice asks. "How do you know? What did he do?"

But all Djamilla will say is that Alice should be careful.

6

I n the big black-and-white bathroom, Alice hesitates for a moment, looking down at her phone. She feels she has really no
choice. She tries the number Djamilla has given her. Someone
answers almost immediately, speaking in French with what
sounds like a heavy Russian accent. "Who is this?" he asks stiffly
when she says hello.

She asks if it would be possible to talk to him in person. She
needs some information.

"What information?" he asks.

She hesitates for a moment. The voice, though it is heavily
accented, the French halting and uncertain, still sounds vaguely
familiar. Alice decides to tell the truth. She says she is Michel's
wife, Alice de Sevigné, and she is trying to find out what happened to her husband. "I believe you were one of his clients and
with him the day he disappeared."

"If you want information you would have to come here to me,
and make sure you were not followed by anyone. No police," he
says firmly. *Pas de police!* He insists.

"And where might that be? Where would I have to come?"
Alice asks.

He says he is at sea on a boat.

"On the *Élysée*?"

"Yes, not far from Ventimiglia. You would have to come to
the boat."

"Italy? I would have to come to Italy? Why Italy?" she asks.

"Italy is safer—contacts here."

"And you expect me to come to you there?"

He says, "Yes. Necessary. I cannot come to you. I can give you the information you need. I will anchor briefly in a bay. I will tell you exactly how to find the boat. You will have to swim out to me. Your husband mentioned that you are an unusually strong swimmer; is that true?"

"I am a good swimmer," Alice admits.

"I need to make certain no one is following. I can't come too close. They are looking for the boat. Do you understand?" the man asks.

"You expect me to actually swim out to you! You are asking a great deal of me," Alice says, wondering how this man could demand such a thing.

"The information I have will be worth it. It is very important to you and your daughter." He pauses for a moment, as if waiting for her to say something, and when she doesn't he goes on. "If you want to know how your husband died, you must come as soon as possible."

Alice is still not sure what to say, but he apparently presumes she will do as he asks. "Call me when you get to Ventimiglia and I will give you exact directions to the boat—remember, above all, no police." There is something about this voice, a certain strange authority, as if the man were convinced she would do what he asked, that makes Alice feel she should do what he has proposed, outrageous as it seems.

Before she does anything else, though, she decides to book a seat on a plane back to America for Pamela. She wants to make sure her darling girl, at least, is safe. She will send her to Lizzie. She calls Lizzie and speaks to her briefly to tell her that Pamela is safe. Can she take care of her for Alice for a few days? Alice is planning on coming home soon after a brief trip to Italy.

"Italy? Why Italy?" Lizzie asks.

Alice promises to explain all soon. She says she will send Pamela to her tomorrow and she herself is planning to come home Friday, if all goes well.

7

They leave the hotel in Lugano early to drop Pamela at the airport with her backpack and her passport, which the school has sent to them by express mail. She is flying via Zurich to New York's JFK, where Lizzie will come and pick her up. Pamela clings to her mother at the last minute, reluctant to let her go. The girl leaves her with tears streaming down her face, and it takes all of Alice's resolve to give her a last hug and tell her to go. Alice stands waving and watching her go through customs for as long as she can see her. Pamela has reclaimed her old stuffed lamb, which she holds against her cheek. Alice feels the tears in her eyes, watching her poor child, who she can see has regressed to an earlier stage of her life for some sort of comfort, clinging to this old, grubby toy and surreptitiously sucking her thumb from time to time.

Alice's heart breaks for Pamela, who seems sometimes so grown-up and wise, bright and knowing, vacillating on the threshold of adulthood, yet anxious and reluctant to take the step. While they have been together she has watched with sorrow as her daughter seemed to regress to an earlier time of her life, not letting her mother out of her sight and sleeping beside her in the hotel bed. Now she has to send her off on her own to be safe with her sister.

Alice feels she cannot endanger her daughter's life again by taking her with her to Italy. She is too terrified of being led astray by this Russian, and yet she feels somehow she has no choice but to go herself. She has to find out what happened. She needs to know the truth about Michel's death.

PART XI

Amagansett

Late September
Tuesday

I

$\mathcal{L}$IZZIE

1

At Kennedy airport, Lizzie and Sergei stand side by side, anxiously watching the passengers on the flight from Zurich pass through the gate, looking for Pamela. Lizzie watches as a young girl in blue jeans comes striding forth, a leather backpack that she recognizes as Alice's on her back.

"There she is," Lizzie says, and calls out her name, waving her arms. Pamela's face lights up as she sees her aunt. Lizzie hugs her niece, holding on to her and telling her she is so happy to see her. "Look at you! So tall! So grown-up! So beautiful! Where is my little niece?" Pamela seems to have grown a foot in the four months since Lizzie saw her last, at the beginning of the summer, before everything began. She looks so slender and tall in her blue jeans and a blue shirt, with her smooth pink-and-white skin, her thick blond hair flying in loose locks behind her. She smiles her big smile at her aunt—they must be almost the same height, Lizzie thinks, and hugs her again.

Pamela's dark eyes shine with tears. "I'm so glad to be here with you finally! I missed you so much!" she says.

Sergei kisses her on both pink cheeks and gives her a big grin, telling her he is so happy she is safe and sound. "We were worried about you," he says, and Lizzie can see it in his eyes.

"I want to hear everything, everything! What happened? Why did you leave school? Where did you go?" Lizzie says, putting an arm around her shoulder. "Are you all right, darling? You look exhausted—sad?" she asks, seeing the tears in her niece's dark eyes, the dark rings beneath them.

"I couldn't sleep on the plane—just so worried about Mommy. I wish she had let me go with her."

Lizzie says, "Well, I'm glad you are here with us, darling, safe and sound."

Sergei takes Pamela's backpack and strides ahead, leading them to the parking lot where he has left his old white car. He makes Pamela sit in the front beside him in the Jaguar—so that he can see her, he says, as if she might disappear again. And indeed he turns to her repeatedly as he drives, making Lizzie, who sits in the back, nervous. Sergei is a fast driver who always makes her nervous when he is driving.

This afternoon, however, driving to the country house on the Long Island Expressway, the road is congested; they are unable to drive fast. The sky seems low and gray. The afternoon air is cool.

Both Lizzie and Sergei question Pamela, and she tells them some of her story, but she seems more anxious to question them. She says she was carried off by some people who brought her to a house not far from Lugano. She is not sure what these people were doing there or why, but they interrogated her and thought she might know something about the secret account of a Russian man her father was going to meet on his boat. They wanted to access his money.

She thinks they were probably Russians, from the accent, she says. "Do you know if they could have been Russian?" she asks Sergei.

He replies, "Yes, quite probably. Lots of Russians in that area."

"Why?" Pamela asks.

"Some of them were engaged in money laundering. They had brought enormous amounts of gold from Saint Petersburg that was melted down in Lugano."

"Gold?" Pamela says.

Sergei nods his head.

"No one said anything about that. I think they were looking for this Russian my father knew, because he had money they wanted and they thought I might know how to locate the secret number and name of the account." She explains that her mother has gone to Italy to meet him, the man who was supposed to meet her father on the boat.

"So that's why she is going to Italy," Lizzie says. "Goodness!"

"I'm so worried this man might hurt her in some way. What if he's dangerous? Do you know anything about him? Was he a client of my father's?" Pamela asks Sergei, biting a nail.

He nods his head again and says, "It's quite possible. I did introduce your father to a wealthy Russian who had recently become a client and who seems to have disappeared." Lizzie anxiously hopes he doesn't tell her niece anything too frightening about him.

"Your mother is such a practical woman, darling," Lizzie says, leaning forward and interrupting. "I'm sure she wouldn't do anything foolish. She never has. She was always the careful one—unlike me. I was always the one who took the closed ski runs. She was the prudent one, making umpteen turns down the slopes." She smiles at her niece, who turns to her in the car, though she does wonder what Alice is thinking and why she has risked this voyage to Italy to meet an unknown and possibly dangerous man, leaving her daughter to travel alone.

Pamela asks Sergei about the Russian client. "Who is he? Who is this man?"

"Nickname was Spera—like hope, you know. Did you do any Latin at school?"

"A little bit," Pamela says.

"Anyway, that's what they called him. One of Putin's old friends, I believe. I don't know what his real name is."

"What's he like?" Pamela asks.

Sergei seems to be thinking about what to respond and eventually says, "Very intelligent man, very rich—like most of those who have remained friends with Vovka."

"Vovka?" Lizzie asks.

"Vladimir Putin. One of those bright boys who sit on the toilet and read chess books and forget where they are—if you see what I mean. He and Vovka were both law students in Leningrad, and eventually both in the *cheka*, the KGB—they may have even been in Dresden together. Anyway, like your father he speaks several languages—fluent German, French. Friendly man with a face like a choirboy—charming, I thought when I met him."

"How did he get so rich?" Pamela asks.

"The KGB really created the oligarchs, you might say, but then they lost control. First he was in what they called the active reserves, a post without a salary but with access to information—agents with information about what they called black money, illegal money which flooded abroad. Some of it went to Switzerland, as almost everyone else's foreign money did, too, avoiding taxes."

"How did you meet him?" Pamela wants to know.

"I was invited to his house not too far from yours, actually, when I was staying with you in early June. A grand house, though rather garish—lots of gold. He was—is—such an interesting man, or seemed so; very proud of his Russian heritage, always talking about Shostakovich, who was a great favorite. Very well dressed, designer clothes, drove fast cars. Knew loads of people. Gave lavish parties."

"Could he have known these people who kidnapped me? The people in the house where they kept me? The ones that were looking for him?" Pamela asks.

"It is possible, I'm afraid. He had all sorts of business connections. Always entertaining. At the time I was trying to be helpful. I thought he might be a good client for your father," Sergei says as he weaves between the cars, driving fast now along the expressway.

Lizzie says, "Well, he doesn't sound very dangerous, darling," though she thinks the contrary. "And perhaps he can put your mother's mind at rest," she says to Pamela, as Sergei turns, finally, down the long driveway, passing under the big magnolia tree and approaching the blue door.

"Here we are! Finally home! Thank goodness!" Lizzie says with relief. She jumps out the moment Sergei stops the car to find the key in the box where they left it Sunday before returning to the city.

2

It is already twilight as they go inside, carrying Lizzie's heavy bags from the grocery store in Brooklyn where she shopped for their dinner and the days they are planning to spend out here. She has promised to make dinner that evening for Sergei and Pamela. Lizzie, who never cooked when she and Alice lived together, has turned out to be surprisingly good at it.

When they have deposited her bags on the kitchen table and put away the food, Lizzie strides around the big rooms to make sure all is in order, showing Pamela around the old house, which she has not seen for several years.

"You can sleep upstairs in the big bedroom, where your mother slept, if you like," Lizzie says.

Pamela says she doesn't mind where she sleeps. The small bedroom is fine; she is just happy to be here with them in this house she remembers from her early childhood.

"It all seems exactly the way I remember it—even the smell of apples," she comments, sniffing the air with its faint scent from the big silver bowl of apples on the mahogany table in the dining room. Lizzie looks around at the two silver candelabra shining on the upright studio Steinway; the threadbare oriental carpets, which have been vacuumed; and the three yellow pillows, which are propped up in their usual places on the big worn leather sofa.

Thanks to Alice's money, Rosa has been here, Lizzie sees, putting all to rights. *What a luxury!* she thinks. She gets Sergei to
help her bring up some logs from the basement to lay the fire in
the big fireplace. She considers herself an expert fire maker, having learned how to do this in Girl Scouts when she was at the
Quaker school in New York. Now she shows Pamela how to lay
a fire, putting down the newspaper, propping the wood up so
that the air can circulate underneath, placing the twigs vertically
to catch the fire. She lights a match, stands back, and admires the
blaze. The fireplace has always drawn well, and the wood is dry.
She wants to make the house as warm and welcoming as possible
for her niece.

It is still warm out, an Indian summer, the sky clear now at
the end of the day. They have not yet turned on the heat in the
house, though the pool has been covered over, she sees through
the French doors. No one wanted to pay for unnecessary pool
service at this point. Sergei is out in the yard picking up branches
and twigs from the lawn.

She is so glad Sergei has come with her, and she wants to
question him further about this Russian whom Alice has gone
to see. She is happy to hear he has been making inquiries and that
he seems to even know the man and speaks well of him, though
she suspects he has not told Pamela all he knows. He has seemed
preoccupied recently, working until late in the evening so that
Lizzie has hardly seen him, and when she has, he has been muttering mysteriously about his colleagues. How much does he
know about these people who kidnapped her niece? she wonders. How involved is he with them? Will she ever know?

Pamela stands in the middle of the big room, looking at

Lizzie's paintings on the walls. She says, "You always said each chair is someone in the family, right?"

Lizzie smiles and nods her head. "You have a good memory."

Pamela asks her to tell her who is who. She wants to know which chair represents her mother.

"She's this one," Lizzie says, pointing out the big bold blue-and-white-striped chair, with its straight arms and legs. "Your mother was so important to me all my life. After our mother died, I followed her around like a little lost shadow. I wouldn't let her out of my sight. I copied all she did, pretending I could read when she could but just remembering the words by heart. She taught me all I know. She was the one, really, who instilled the need to be disciplined, to work hard, to follow my conscience, to do the right thing."

"And which one is you, Aunt Lizzie? Did you do yourself?"

"This one was me," she tells her niece, pointing out the yellow Louis Quinze chair, with its curved legs and arms. She has included herself in the chair portraits.

"The prettiest one," Pamela says. "Mommy always says you were the prettier sister, with your blond hair and blue eyes. You were always the sweetest, too, she said, and the lively one, the brightest in the family. I think I like that one best," Pamela adds, and gives her aunt a hug.

Lizzie says, "I was only five when your grandmother died, but I can see myself as I was then—maybe I've seen a photograph, with my fat, red cheeks and unruly curls, angry blue eyes, spot on my dress. I remember feeling angry that life had been so unfair. I suppose that in a way, the time before Mother's death, though I don't remember much of it, has always seemed like a sort of lost paradise so that nothing in the present is ever quite what those years were, lit up with a sort of glow."

As she speaks to her niece, Lizzie wonders if Tolstoy's famous first sentence about happy families all being alike is correct. Surely people are happy in very different ways, though it may be more difficult to write novels about happy families than unhappy ones. Were they a happy family until her mother died? Has she given those few years a retrospective glow in her mind that they did not really deserve?

"And Grandpa?" Pamela asks. "Which one is he?"

She points to the painting of the big green curved Matisse-looking chair in the center. "I suppose I thought of him as the center of our world. He was so tall. I remember once, I must have been very little, not long after Mother's death, telling my sister not to let my father pick me up from kindergarten. She asked me why not, and I said, 'He's too tall.' He was very handsome, and an excellent musician, though never a famous one. He could do it all, conduct as well as play so many instruments: the piano as well as the violin and even the oboe. Your mother inherited his musical gifts."

Lizzie remembers how her father would say laughingly, "The three K's: Khachaturian, Klemperer, and Konrad." He loved the good things in life: music, art, books, good conversation, good food and wine. She always felt he was interested in what she had to say even as a child. But it was their mother who was the consistent one, until she died. Their father gave his girls their love of art.

"This one was Mother," Lizzie says, pointing out the small fragile chair. "She died so young, so surprisingly, when I was so little, leaving your mother in charge."

Looking at her paintings, Lizzie asks herself if they will last, if what she has spent so many hours of her life doing has been worth all the effort. She loves the process of painting, loves looking at paintings, always attempting to learn something new from others, but should she rather have done something that would have helped others more than she has done?

She looks at her niece's face, her dark sad eyes. What can she do for this fatherless child? she wonders. What if anything were to happen to Alice? What if she never comes back?

Pamela says, "I think your paintings are beautiful, Aunt Lizzie. You are so lucky to have your art."

"We were both lucky, your mother and I. We must get her to play for us when she arrives. She left her violin here in the house."

3

Later that night when Pamela is asleep in the small bedroom next door, Lizzie questions Sergei about the Russian her sister is supposed to meet.

"Who is this man?" she asks.

"I'm not sure, but he may actually be connected to the Russian Mafia. Many of these oligarchs are. I think he came from a rough background. He's not a huge guy, but he looked pretty wiry and strong to me. He mentioned he'd done judo. He seemed very brilliant, spoke a lot of languages, and obviously had a good ear, like Michel, and I think he liked music. It seems to me we talked about art—always a safe subject."

"You talked about art?" Lizzie says.

"His activities came under scrutiny at one point, they told me, when too much money began to disappear abroad. All kinds of shady transactions: fictitious real estate acquisitions, fabrication of fake art—much of the Russian avant-garde art is fake—factories run by Russian crime syndicates, stealing and reselling of cars, production of fake hard liquor. You name it, he seems to have done it."

"Good heavens!"

"He seems to have been responsible for some sort of Russian-Swiss joint venture with or without Putin's blessing. Most of these oligarchs would go through Geneva en route to wherever they were going. No one refused their money, of course. I don't know all the details, but I do remember being at his grand house in Nice for a party, and getting up to find the bathroom after drinking too much champagne. I got lost in the labyrinth of rooms and long corridors and just walked by chance into a smoky room where several men sat around a table. One of them had a gun on the table in front of him."

"Good heavens," Lizzie says again, appalled.

"Spera may very well be connected with this group who must have picked up poor Pamela. He probably owed them money and they were trying to track down the number of his bank account and thought the girl might know where to find it. I was furious when I heard about it! Thank goodness she managed to escape. She's a plucky girl."

"And now, Alice!" Lizzie says. "What might happen to her?"

Sergei just looks at her and shakes his head. "I wish she had consulted me before going off to meet the man. I don't know what she thinks he can tell her!"

PART XII

ITALY

Tuesday

I

ALICE

1

Alice crosses the border into Italy and stops the car at the side of the road. She takes out her cell phone and listens to the clear and precise directions to the bay where the Russian has promised to meet her. She is not a confident driver—Michel always did the driving when they were together—and she drives painfully slowly, wiping her glasses from time to time. She thinks of Pamela, wonders once again if she is safe alone. She imagines her on the airplane worried and longing for her mother, her father—though, of all the people in the world, Lizzie is the one Alice feels happiest about caring for her daughter. She imagines her sister holding Pamela in her arms. Lizzie loves her as if she were her own. If anything should happen to Alice, she knows Lizzie would step in and take her place, as Alice once did for their mother.

The heavy traffic on the narrow road, the reckless Italian drivers, who pass when they should not, even the low sky, which seems to hang heavy above her, all add to her anxiety. Alice, who is usually so polite to strangers, finds herself swearing aloud in Italian at the other drivers, as though they could hear her. "*Stronzo*," she mutters as a car pulls out in front of her suddenly, though she is not quite sure what the word means.

She follows the winding coastal route, only stopping at one point to go into a store and buy a sandwich for lunch. She forces the bread and ham down her throat, drinks some orange juice like it's medicine, afraid of fainting.

She stops the car about a mile outside the town at the side of the road near the small bay the man indicated. It is late afternoon, the air cool. Rain threatens. She remembers coming to Ventimiglia with Michel and Pamela years ago, when Pamela was quite small.

She leaves all her belongings—her phone, her watch, her glasses, and her shoes—in the trunk of the car, in her small suitcase, taking only the keys to the car. She finds the exit from the road with difficulty. She has put her swimsuit on under her dress. She walks barefoot down the sandy path to the small rocky gray beach the man described. Has she not been here before? she wonders, looking around. Something seems familiar; a sudden recollection of Michel with Pamela on his shoulders running along the edge of the beach, the water splashing around his feet, the sun shining on Pamela's blond hair, comes to her with a deep ache of loss and longing.

The place seems deserted. One gnarled and leaning tree shelters a side of the cove, and beneath the tree she sees an overturned yellow plastic bucket some child must have abandoned in the sand.

The water is calm. She stands at the edge and looks across the bay for the boat the man has told her will be there. She sees nothing but the sea stretching on endlessly to the horizon. She lifts her hands to her forehead, straining her eyes to see without her glasses. She wonders if she has come to the right place or if she should go back and get her phone and call the Russian.

Then, in the distance she sees a boat approaching that she does not recognize, a blue boat. Alice can see it slowly coming closer to the shore. Only the jib is up, swelling in the slight breeze. Someone drops anchor at least a mile out from the shore.

She stares at the shapely hull and light wood trim and realizes now that this is Michel's boat, the *Élysée*, though the color has changed. How could this have happened? she wonders. Is it lawful to change the color of a boat? How has the man acquired it, the papers, changed its color? Has he murdered Michel and now intends to do the same to her?

Moments from their times on the boat Michel loved come to her mind. She sees herself lying by his side on the deck, rocking in his arms, the stars winking at a pallid moon; drinking a glass of white wine in the evening with the boat anchored safely, waves lapping at the hull; the ropes rattling against the mast; the illusion that such happiness can last forever.

Such a beautiful boat, she thinks, standing on the shore and looking at the lilt of it now with longing, a boat Michel loved so much, a large part of the pleasure in his life. Sometimes he would say, looking at her strangely, that he could imagine just taking off sailing to the horizon on his own. How sad he would be to see his boat has changed color and is in someone else's hands. Why can the man not come in closer? And can she swim that far?

2

She watches a gray gull swoop down low over the water and wonders how foolish this is, plunging into the sea and swimming such a distance. And even if she can swim the distance, what might happen on the boat with this unknown man? If he killed Michel, why would he have consented to talk to her? she wonders. A murderer would hardly have anything to say to his victim's wife, unless he were a particularly perverse man. There is nothing she can do for him, surely—but what might he do to her? Will he ask her for money? But apparently he is a rich man, with his money still hidden in a secret bank account: Speranski. She remembers the name Pamela told her. Yet this man knows the secret of Michel's death, she is certain.

She tells herself the only way to find out is to swim to the boat. She is a good, strong swimmer, she believes. She never really feels tired when she is swimming. If she is going to do it, she should not wait any longer. The evening can only get colder and darker at this point, she thinks, looking up at the low gray sky. She has come this far, after all, sent her daughter off on her own, because it seems to be the only way she will ever find out what has happened to Michel.

She pulls off her dress, lifting it over her head, so that for a moment she is blinded before she stands shivering on the edge of the shore. She kicks the dress to one side, then bends down and shovels some sand over it so that it will not be blown away or picked up by some tramp. She tucks her car keys between her breasts, down the front of her swimsuit, and wades into the water.

Was she at fault? Alice wonders once again, feeling the cool water rise to her calves. Did Michel want to die in the water? Was he destroyed by the letter Luigi had sent her? Was it his work, the lack of clients, the atmosphere at the bank, that had driven him to despair? Or was there some kind of foul play? She needs to know, for her own peace of mind, but she thinks of what curiosity can do to the curious, and how Oedipus was blinded for looking for a truth he would surely have preferred not to know. What if this man tells her something she would rather not hear?

Alice looks at the still, gray sea and wonders now as the water rises to her waist if there's a current in the water. If there is, she'll lie on her back and let herself drift. She will drift either out to the boat or toward the shore.

Faintly in the distance Alice seems to see a figure standing at the prow of the boat. The figure waves and she waves back. From that distance she cannot see his face or even much of his form, but he does not seem to be tall or particularly large. There is nothing menacing about him. He seems to be wearing white boating clothes like Michel's the day he died—like a ghost, she thinks.

Then she pushes forward, lifting her feet from the ground. She swims fast in the cold water, doing a strong seagoing crawl, lifting her head up from time to time to make sure she is going in the right direction, the water clouding her eyes. She does not seem to be advancing. She has the impression the boat is moving away. Is she being lured onward to her death? There are no other boats in the bay where she could stop to rest on the way if she had to. There is no one watching who might help her. She thinks of her child now, how precious she is, and how she is all that is left to Pamela. What will the child do if something happens to her mother? Alice wonders. She has promised her she will call her as soon as she can, but will she ever reach this boat, which is now so strangely blue? Rather than approaching, the boat seems to be drawing away, luring her farther and farther away from the shore. When she looks up she tries to make out the letters on the side of the boat, the name. It, too, seems to have changed. This blue boat is no longer called the *Élysée*, she realizes. Is she dreaming? The name she sees painted in white letters is *Circe*, and next to it there is a sort of painted mermaid. She tries to recall who Circe was. Vaguely she remembers. Wasn't Circe the one who did something bad to Odysseus or to his men? Was she the magic one who turned them into swine?

3

There must be some current in the water, Alice realizes as she struggles on, trying to swim toward the boat. She swims more and more slowly, cramps going all the way up her legs, her arms; under her ribs, her heart seems to be cramping. Is it possible? She has no more strength left. Alice looks back longingly now at the gray stony beach, but she cannot retreat; it is no longer possible—she could not make the return to the shore. She is breathless and giddy, and her whole body is cramping in the cold water, but she presses on.

She can see the man on the boat is waving her on and shouting something to her, which at first she cannot understand. Is he calling her name?

She tries to keep swimming, or at least to lift her head out of the water, though she can hardly move her legs, her arms. Her name comes to her now as if in a dream. Someone is calling her: "Alice! Alice!" Someone is beckoning to her from the dead; she recognizes the voice, a voice she knows so well, a voice she loves, has always loved, calling her name. She must be dreaming—or is she dying and going to join the one she loves more than any other in the underworld? She lifts her head and through the blur of water and tears in her eyes, she sees who it is, and why he has asked her to come. She is not surprised. Perhaps she has known this all along, sensed that the body she saw in the morgue was not his, for it is Michel who is standing on the boat, clapping his hands like a child, and now with the last of her strength she is able to reach up and grasp the bottom rung of the ladder. It is Michel who leans down to grasp her hand, her arm, to drag her body up the steps, Michel who is not dead but alive, his face sunburned, his body thin, Michel who folds her trembling body in his arms.

II

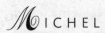

1

"Alice," he says, holding her wet limp body against his own. She has always been thin, but now it seems to him that he can feel only her bones—her ribs, her hip bones, her thighbones—against his body. There seems hardly anything left of her. What has he done to her? He remembers once going through customs with her and how a customs official had thought one of her ribs was a gun.

She says nothing to him, just staring at him with disbelief, anger in her eyes.

"I almost drowned!"

He shakes his head and says, "But you made it!"

She stands back from him on the deck. "What happened?" she asks as Michel puts a towel around her shoulders, his arm encircling her waist as he helps her tenderly down the steps into the cabin, where she collapses. She is shivering, her teeth chattering, and she seems to have difficulty breathing. She has swum all this way to find out about him. Michel is afraid she might faint here in the cabin before he can warm her and explain what has happened. He takes a bottle of red wine from under the stove, removes the cork, and pours her a big glass.

"Drink this. It will warm you," he says, handing her the glass and then finding some blankets to cover her trembling limbs. She drinks and shakes her head at him, obviously bewildered by a rush of conflicting emotions.

He looks at her and tries to read her expression. Is she glad to see him alive, or in a rage? How can he explain what has occurred?

"Why did you make me swim so far?" she asks angrily. She adds, "Do you know what has happened to Pamela?"

"Is she all right?" he asks.

Alice just nods her head. "She is now!"

"An ugly business," Michel says, not looking at her. "Rest for a while. You must rest and eat and drink first, and then I will try and tell you what happened."

PART XIII

BEAULIEU-SUR-MER

August

I

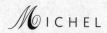ICHEL

1

The wind has risen as Michel and the Russian stand side by side in the bright light, contemplating the water. The sun glints blindingly on the choppy sea. Michel thinks he is going to die without having ever lived properly. His heart pains him, his breath comes with difficulty, and he feels heavy, the weight of his whole meaningless life on his shoulders, this life he has dragged like a boulder with him all these years to this moment on the boat standing beside this man. If he could only free himself from this burden!

The wind blows the waves against the side of the boat. As Michel struggles with the load of his whole life, the boom, which he has not bothered to attach, swings suddenly in the wind and knocks the Russian off-balance. Michel stands there unmoving, watching as the man is flung suddenly backward into the sea, falling so easily, tumbling like a limp doll over the side of the boat in a way Michel has always thought would be the best way to die.

For a moment he cannot move. He just stands there watching the man go down and down into the blue depths. He waits for the Russian to come back up to the surface, but nothing happens, and soon Michel realizes he must have been hurt, perhaps by the blow of the heavy beam against his head. He does not emerge. He is down there falling and falling.

The Russian sinks like a stone, without a struggle. He must, Michel realizes, be concussed. Then, without thinking, he takes a great breath of air, diving down into the sea. Afterward he is not certain if he wanted to save the man or to drown himself, to go down with the Russian. Down, down Michel goes until he grasps the man's body and they continue on together, entwined. Michel holds on to the Russian's body as if it could save him. They will lie together in the depths of the sea. Together they go down until they reach the sandy bottom.

Michel just holds the Russian in his arms tightly. He isn't a big man; in fact he is almost exactly Michel's size and not too heavy, which Michel has already noticed, of course. His clothes would fit this man perfectly.

Michel is not certain who should die. What difference would it make in the end? Should they both die? Could he leave the man here or can he drag him slowly back up, making sure he is dead, that he is no longer breathing, that he is inert? He could take his place.

It occurs to Michel in that instant, with the flickering underwater light in his eyes, how easily he could change his life, throw off the burden of his own past. He realizes he does not want to die; he just does not want to live this life, his life, and that this thought has been there in his mind, perhaps since the first moment he met this man. He does not have to be the one to die. He can take on a new identity and with it a new freedom. He can escape a life that has grown useless and sad. He can escape in his beloved boat. He must get the man back up onto the boat.

What proves harder is to drag the Russian's body back onto the deck, harder than going down into the depths with him. But the ladder is there, and with a great struggle, Michel is able to lift the body over the side of the boat and onto the deck. Gasping for air, he staggers up himself. He stands for a moment shaking in the sunshine, looking at the Russian's body lying before him. Michel feels light, unburdened, alive, a free man, free to roam, to take off alone in his boat, to start anew.

Quickly, he makes the switch of the clothes, dresses the Russian in his own shirt and trousers, puts his cards and wallet in the pocket, as well as his gold watch on the man's arm.

Then he just lets the body go back into the water. He feels as if he is saying good-bye to himself, to his own past as he watches this familiar body, now dressed in his own clothes, sink slowly. He knows the sea will do its disguising work—no fingerprints, no way really to know who this man is without a DNA test, and why would anyone do that? How long will it take to find the body? Days, surely, perhaps even weeks.

Then he lifts the ladder and the anchor, tightens the sails, and takes off. He knows he is leaving Alice and his daughter, but he has provided for them, he thinks. They will be happier without him. They will go on with their lives; Alice will go back to Luigi. He has sufficient food and water on the boat for several days and he knows how to stay away from the coast and the coast guard.

PART XIV

VENTIMIGLIA

September

I

ᴬLICE

1

It is not until she has lingered long in the hot, steamy shower, until Michel has rubbed her aching calves and arms with grease, dried her salty hair, not until he has grilled her sardines under the stars the way he used to do, not until they have drunk several glasses of cheap chianti and Alice has told Michel about Pamela, how she is, how she found her sleeping behind the sofa in the hotel in Lugano, curled up and dusty in her navy skirt, that Michel tells Alice his story.

They sit side by side on the deck in the mysterious light of the moon, with the stars above them, in the shadows on the boat cushions, covered with blankets, and Michel looks at Alice and tells her, "I've killed a man."

"Not possible!" she exclaims.

He shakes his head. "Who would have thought such a thing possible? Who would have considered I of all people could do such a thing? But I have."

"The Russian?" Alice asks, and he nods his head.

"It was self-defense? He attacked you on the boat? He tried to take money from you? You tried to defend yourself? You had to kill him." She has already made up a plausible scenario in her mind.

He shakes his head. "Not entirely." He sighs and adds, "More, I'm afraid the police would say, if it came to a trial, premeditated murder. Something that had been running through my mind like a constant and underground stream, like a dream, vivid, plausible, possible, planned, and yet impossible. Until the last moment I never thought I could or would do it."

Alice stares at him and asks, "Is it possible, Michel?"

He explains: "He was just one of those stupid men simmering with a sort of natural nastiness—a man not worthy of being alive, a liar and a cheat."

She stares at him.

"I told you about him. He was introduced to me as a wealthy Saint Petersburg businessman, a possible client. Apparently he had held a high position in Russia at one time, KGB, had worked for German Gref. A lawyer; seemed so smart. I liked him so much."

Michel goes on explaining.

"My life seemed so useless—my work pointless. Things I had been so proud of had now become suspect. I'd kept so many secrets uselessly. Now everything was exposed. I had no longer any feeling of worth. I think the Russian had gone through something similar when the Soviet Union came to an end, and he came back from Germany in 1990."

Alice is not sure what to say and just stares at Michel.

"And even you, Alice?" He looks at her so sorrowfully in the moonlight with his wide-spaced eyes, and tells her when he found the letter from Luigi, he was undone. "It was not so much the letter itself but the fact that it was such a *good* love letter full of poetry, lovely lines filled with hope—a letter from a young, budding musician, someone who loved what you loved, understood you, loves you. I felt you belonged with him."

"But I never belonged with him, Michel! How could I have? Such a young man starting out in his life. Ten years younger. Not much more than thirty years old. Besides he told me he'd been one of Sergei's lovers. We would never, could never have stayed together," she says, looking at his face in the shadows. "We were a family, you and I. You were part of my life."

"I felt you were no longer my home, my heart, Alice. You had found joy, happiness, music with someone else."

Alice cannot deny the truth of what he says. "You were such a good husband to me, Michel, always, such a good father—the best. We had so many happy moments. Didn't we come here once, to this bay with Pamela when she was very little?"

Michel nods his head. "That's why I chose it—I came as close as I could. I wondered if you would remember."

"Of course I remembered. And yet you made me almost drown coming to get you!" she says, glaring at him, remembering her panic in the water.

He says, "I would have come to your rescue if it were necessary."

"Perhaps, though in that case we would probably both have drowned. I actually swim much better than you do; you know perfectly well—and then what would poor Pamela have done?"

"Ah, Pamela!" he says. "Darling Pamela growing up, going on with her young life. She was so happy at boarding school with her friends, her teachers, as she should have been. She was hovering on the brink of becoming a restless teenager. What does she need me for?"

"But children need us all their lives."

"We used to be so close. I couldn't bear to lose her, to lose you, my work. I felt you would all be better off without me and with some money. You needed money—for her school, for your work, the villa—more than me."

"That's nonsense! That's not true!" she says angrily.

"The final insult was when the bank began talking about taking away the boat," he says. "It was no longer necessary. They needed to cut back. They had already cut my salary considerably. I could imagine my life without my work, without you, even without Pamela, but not without the freedom of my boat. That was when I doubled the life insurance, or rather death insurance, told Djamilla where I kept my blue book, told her what to say, ordered her to go home when I was no more, when Pamela was back at school. I was contemplating ending my life on the boat. Of course she protested vehemently. She was furious."

Then in May, or early June, at his lowest moment, he met the Russian, Spera—or the man who called himself that, Michel tells her, which turned out to be a fake name. "His friends called him Spera, which seemed a good name for him—such a cheerful man. Baby-faced, he seemed, well . . . innocent."

"Innocent?"

"He was full of charm, the way only the Russians can be. So sincere, it seemed to me, generous with his friends, good-hearted, or so I thought."

Michel explains how he had a lot of time on his hands. Alice was distracted, distant, Pamela still off at school. They met often, talked about the meaning of life.

"We drank together—the Russians, you know, really like to drink. I was drinking too much. We talked about women; I even told him about you and Luigi, the letter," Michel says. He stares up at the sky. "You can imagine the picture." And indeed Alice can, as well as Michel's attraction to someone who had everything he wanted, everything he was losing: his villa, even his beautiful boat.

Michel continues, "It was surprisingly easy. Death, like life, is a surprisingly simple thing, you know, Alice. We are all afraid of it but it happens so quickly, and often by chance. It happened so quickly to him, though afterward, of course, there were unwanted repercussions." He looks out across the moonlit sea.

Alice says nothing, just looking at the moonlight shining on the sea. Nothing is changed in the universe, she thinks. All of this will go on forever, as it has always been, but Michel, though she loves him still—will always love him—is not the man she thought he was. He has deliberately left her and Pamela to face life on their own. He has chosen his own freedom, refused to face his real life with her as a family.

Michel says, "I'm just so sorry, Alice, to have put you through all of this. You and Pamela. I never expected her to be hurt. I was certain she was safely at school. Djamilla had promised she would see her off before she went home. I can't believe they were so negligent. I would love to see her, hold her one last time in my arms, ask for her forgiveness."

"It would be too cruel. It's hard enough for me to be here and know that we will have to part, that you have chosen to leave us.

Perhaps one day you can write to her. I presume you still have access to the money in the secret account. You have to get it to the rest of the Russians, so that they leave us alone. They have frightened her terribly. Understood?"

Michel nods his head. "I will make sure they get what we owe them. Stay a few days with me, darling, will you?" She hesitates, listening to the lap of the water against the boat, feeling the rocking, her anger rising and then subsiding like the sea.

PART XV

AMAGANSETT

Friday Night

I

1

Lizzie keeps looking out the kitchen window to see if Alice has arrived. Her sister telephoned to say she had landed at Kennedy and managed to make the train at Jamaica; she will be here soon. Lizzie wonders what has happened to Alice and also what to say about these days she and Sergei and Pamela have spent together. So many things have occurred. Should she tell her all their news tonight or wait for her to rest?

When Alice finally comes through the front door, she is wearing a smart gray skirt, a turquoise silk shirt, and a matching jacket. Lizzie stands back and watches with pleasure as Pamela throws her arms around her mother, holding on to her. Lizzie laughs with delight, so glad Pamela has her mother back, so glad to see her sister.

"What happened? Did you find the man? What did he say? You said nothing on the phone," Lizzie says.

Alice raises her eyebrows at Lizzie in a warning gesture, and says they should perhaps wait until later for her to tell the story. "Such a strange story! It's hard for me to believe it is real," she says, staring around the big living room. "What is real is this wonderful room and both of you and that I smell dinner!" She laughs and kisses her child again on both her cheeks.

"Chicken and roast potatoes!" Pamela says. "I peeled the potatoes!"

"My favorite! You remembered! Roast potatoes!" Alice says, clapping her hands. "I will tell all after dinner." She throws herself down on the old brown leather sofa, pulling her child down next to her and nuzzling her neck. "I'm just so happy to see you both."

Lizzie sits beside her sister and tells her how delighted they were to have found Pamela at the airport and how they drove out here in Sergei's car. Alice listens so intently as Lizzie speaks, her face lit up by her words and the flickering of the fire Lizzie has laid. Lizzie likes the pink lampshade that hangs above them and casts a soft glow. She likes the high ceiling of this room, which always lifts her heart, the old fan stirring up the air. She wants Alice to come back to this house of her youth, to these people who love and admire her.

"What a beautiful dress. Where did you get it? Someone has been spoiling you," Alice says to Pamela, looking up at Lizzie and fingering the white linen at the bodice with the *broderie anglaise* and the spaghetti straps.

"Sergei bought it for me," Pamela says. He insisted on buying her the beautiful white dress with the full skirt and embroidered bodice at an expensive store in East Hampton.

Sergei has spent the past few days with Lizzie and her niece, spoiling Pamela as if he wished to wipe out all the sadness and terror of the past few weeks from her life with his kindness. He has taken her shopping, buying her dresses. Everything suits her, young and slim as she is—pants, shirts, new shoes, a new yellow leather backpack. The three of them have been out to dinner in Montauk, sitting at a table by the window overlooking the sea and eating oysters and lobster. They have been to the movies in East Hampton, followed by ice cream with sprinkles on the top; they have eaten bacon-and-egg sandwiches for breakfast in the wind on the beach, napkins flying. Sergei has spent hours teaching Pamela to play chess, sitting hunched over the board opposite her at the end of the table in the dining room. He has even taken her horseback riding at a stable he knows in Montauk, letting her canter beside him and Lizzie on the beach.

Lizzie has brushed and braided Pamela's fair hair in a French braid, and threaded some daisies through it. Now Pamela sits smiling beside her mother, her face shining with pleasure.

Sergei comes through the front door with two bottles of wine and greets Alice with joy. "So, so glad you are here! Wonderful to see you!" he says.

They sit around the big dining room table, which Lizzie has set with its green-and-white embroidered tablecloth and the silver candelabra, and the silver bowl in the middle. She has found a few late roses and yellow and white chrysanthemums in the garden for a small centerpiece. As she has done the cooking and set the table, she tells everyone where to sit, putting Sergei at the head by the kitchen, and Alice at the other end near the windows, which open on the yard, with Pamela on one side and herself on the other.

Alice sits down at the head of the table. She looks sad, Lizzie notices, watching her stare around the room with a sort of wonder in her slanting eyes, as though she can hardly believe she is here. She is trembling slightly and tears rise in her gray-green eyes from time to time, which she blinks back. What is going to become of her big sister? Lizzie wonders, and reaches out to touch her hand.

Yet earlier, in the kitchen, she heard Sergei tell Alice, "I've talked to some of the Russian mafiosi involved in this fiasco, and made the matter quite clear. Besides, they have apparently found what they were looking for, the missing money!"

"Glad to hear that!" Alice said.

"I think they have given up on this Speranski chap, anyway. He seems to have disappeared into thin air," Sergei told Alice.

Now Lizzie rises and insists that she will serve the dinner. She tells the others not to move. "Let me do this," she says. "You can clean up. You have been through so much," she says to her sister, going through the swinging door that leads into the kitchen. She brings in the dishes she has prepared, thinking of Alice flying back and forth across the Atlantic to rescue her lost daughter, of Pamela disappearing so dangerously from her Swiss school.

Alice smiles up at her and makes little effort to help her put the food on the table, just watching her as she strides back and forth rapidly, her silver sandals slapping against her heels, bringing in the golden chicken on a silver platter, surrounded by the crisp roast potatoes, the string beans, the silver gravy boat. Lizzie is engrossed in her tasks but hears snatches of the conversation as she comes and goes. She hears Sergei tell Alice they have had a fine time with her daughter.

"She will be a good chess player, I suspect," he says.

They *have* had a fine time, Lizzie thinks. She has taken a few days off teaching to be here with her niece and Sergei. The three of them have been together most of the time. Unexpected things have happened. She wants to prepare Alice for her news. What will she say?

When Lizzie sits down she tells them she is planning on moving in with Sergei. "We would save so much time not having to travel back and forth," she explains shyly, as though this is an entirely practical decision.

Alice laughs and says, "You'll have to learn to be tidy, then!"

Sergei uncorks the champagne he has brought and pours for all. Then he carves the chicken expertly and passes it around.

When everyone is served Lizzie asks her sister to tell her story. "Tomorrow," Alice says, "when I have finally had a good night's sleep."

Sergei, who is sitting opposite Alice at the top of the table with Pamela on his left, turns to the girl and says, filling her glass, "You should have a glass of champagne, too, Pamela. You deserve one. We should celebrate your mother's and your safe return to America. You are a brave girl, and an enterprising one, and I can see very soon you are going to beat me at chess, which will make me mad! Tonight you can sleep soundly and know you and your mother are quite safe now you are both here with us."

Lizzie looks at Pamela in her fresh white dress, sipping her champagne daintily. She sits so upright at the dining room table, only her wrists on the table, and passes the dishes so politely to everyone. Lizzie thinks of Michel and the good manners that were so important to him and that he instilled in his daughter.

She looks at Pamela's round smooth face, such a beautiful face, but the dark eyes are still filled with sadness. Yet Lizzie feels the child has been happy with them over the past few days. How much the girl has suffered, she thinks, and wonders again what she can do to help her. She remembers the paintings they made together when she was younger and how talented Pamela is. She hopes they can draw together again in the clear fall light outside. The light in this area has drawn so many painters, for good reason.

It is wonderful to have her niece and her sister here with them in the old house, Lizzie thinks, wiggling her toes in her sandals under the table. She has forgotten, though, how much work it is to make a complete meal for four people and serve it. There is an apple crumble, which she has chopped and mixed and placed in the oven and will bring forth in due course.

How much should she tell them tonight? she wonders again, looking at her sister and her niece. She can't wait to have Alice's expert advice.

Lizzie sips her champagne and asks Alice where Pamela will go to school now. "I think she has definitely decided to go to school in America, haven't you, darling?" she asks Pamela, hoping the child will be somewhere near, and that they can see her often.

"I certainly don't want to go back to Switzerland," Pamela says.

Alice nods and says, "We will see if we can rent something small in New York, a one-bedroom or even a studio with a loft, probably in the Village—hopefully somewhere near you, if that's where you are going to be—and Pamela can go to school there. We can spend all the holidays out here, hopefully with everyone."

Lizzie thinks of the Quaker school they both attended as girls in the Village. "She should go to the Quakers. We both got such a good education there," she says.

"We'll see where she gets in," Alice says. "It's not as easy as it was when we went to school in the city. It's also so expensive! There's also the French lycée, which is a possibility, or even St. Ann's in Brooklyn."

"I would love it if you were in the Village," Lizzie says, turning to Pamela. "You could come to me for tea after school."

Alice looks proudly at her daughter and says, "Certainly Pamela has good grades and she'll have excellent recommendations, I'm sure, from the school in Switzerland. It's the least they can do!"

Lizzie leans across, takes her niece's hand, and says, "Can I tell them your news, darling? We should celebrate that!"

Pamela shrugs, and smiles a little, flushing, her fresh cheeks turning pink. "Oh, Aunt Lizzie!"

Lizzie says, "Pamela is now officially a woman!" and both sisters smile at her and clap.

"Congratulations!" Alice and Lizzie say in tandem.

"How do you feel about it?" Alice asks her daughter, who shrugs and says so far it just seems a nuisance to her; she keeps looking to see if she has a spot on her skirt. Everyone laughs.

Lizzie says she remembers them celebrating a similar moment in her life in this house when she turned thirteen. "Do you remember?" she asks, and her sister nods.

Alice says, "I remember sitting on the old sofa by the fire and drinking a glass of champagne in your honor—just the two of us."

"You are not eating your chicken," Lizzie says, looking at Alice's plate.

"It's delicious, but I have little appetite," Alice says. Lizzie looks around the table.

Sergei says, "And are you going to tell your sister *your* news?"

Lizzie nods at him and says, "Yes, I have some news for you all, too." They all look at Lizzie, who feels her face flush. She puts her hand to the sapphire flower broach she is wearing on the collar of her blue dress.

"What's happened?" Alice asks. "Good or bad news?"

"I'm not sure if it's good or bad. I suppose it depends on whose point of view you see this from," Lizzie says, smiling and looking at Sergei.

"And from your point of view is it good news?" Alice asks.

"Sergei has asked me to marry him," Lizzie says, smiling at him.

Alice stares at Lizzie and at Sergei, who is grinning. She seems unsure of how to respond.

Lizzie glances at Sergei, who looks exhausted, great rings under his eyes.

"And what have you decided to do?" Alice asks.

Lizzie smiles and says, "I haven't made up my mind. We have both been working too hard. I've been teaching, grading endlessly, and I'm trying to finish my painting. Sergei has had a lot of work, too. We both work too hard." She breaks off but she feels as if she is contemplating something happy. She feels younger, as Alice lifts her hand to stroke Lizzie's blond hair back from her face.

Alice asks, "Did Sergei give you the lovely pin, darling?"

touching the sapphires in the petals of the flower. "Blue, like your eyes?"

Lizzie nods her head. "Who else would it be?"

Alice sighs and says, "No one else."

Pamela grins and looks at Sergei and says, "I know he's got lots of houses, Aunt Lizzie, but don't you think he is rather too old for you? You look so young and beautiful!" Everyone laughs.

Lizzie is trembling all over as she says, "All I know is that life, marvelous and unbearable life's starting up once again."

Alice takes her hand and smiles at her as Pamela reaches across and takes another spoonful of crumble. "And don't forget you are such a good cook, too!" she says.

Alice sighs and says, "In the end there's only food one can count on reliably."

Lizzie looks at her in her shiny silk turquoise shirt. How will she go on without Michel? she wonders. She says, "And music, there is music. You have your music, Alice. Will you play for us before you go to bed, please?"

"I'm too tired tonight," Alice says.

"Oh, please, Mommy. Play the beautiful sonata that I love, the Mozart."

Alice sighs and says she will play the first movement if Pamela will get her violin. And she stands by the fireplace, and they sit around her as she plays for them, back straight, head back, bow lifted, and Lizzie thinks, as she did as a child, that there is something magical about Alice that enables her to make such music. Where do they come from, these notes that blossom like flowers in the air? Where did she get this gift that makes Lizzie's spine tingle and the hair rise up on her arms?

She remembers now how they stood side by side at their mother's grave and watched as they shoveled the earth onto the coffin, how a thunderstorm broke out and it began to rain hard as they stood there so fearfully, so alone, holding each other's hands.

Now Alice says, putting her violin back into its case, "Come on, time for bed—it's about three in the morning for us—say good night, darling," and takes Pamela by the hand. Pamela stands up and bows to the company. "Good night, ladies and gentleman!" she says, blowing a kiss to all with mock theatricality, her dark eyes laughing, her blond plait falling over her shoulder.

She will be fine, Lizzie thinks. Whatever has happened, she will be fine, the beloved child.

As Alice leads her daughter, now officially a young woman, away across the living room and up the stairs into the big bedroom, Lizzie hears Alice telling her not to forget to brush her teeth.

Alice reemerges from the big bedroom where she intends to sleep with Pamela in the double bed, though later when Lizzie climbs out of bed and comes down the stairs she finds Alice on the old sofa. Lizzie will climb up beside her in the dark, and Alice will say, "Pamela?" thinking Lizzie is her daughter, but accepting the affectionate lie when Lizzie says, "Yes."

Now the two sisters sit on the big sofa side by side with Sergei in the armchair by the fire, and Alice tells them her story.

$\mathcal{A}$CKNOWLEDGMENTS

I would like to acknowledge and thank the bankers who read this book for me and those who consented to be interviewed; the writers who portrayed the banking and particularly the world of Russian power and finance so vividly: Karen Dawisha, Bill Browder; Masha Gessen; Luke Harding; Joris Luyendijk; Vladimir Putin; Greg Smith.

Thanks go, too, to the women writers who wrote about sisters and who inspired me, and particularly to Colette.

Much love and thanks go to the sisters in my family: my three daughters and my granddaughters who read and commented so helpfully.

I am very grateful to my agent, Robin Straus, who worked so diligently on this book, and to my editor at Penguin, Kathryn Court, for her guidance and support once again with a new book.

Love and thanks as always to my husband for his encouragement and advice over these many years and many books.

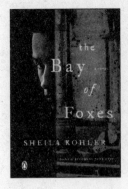  

THE BAY OF FOXES

BECOMING JANE EYRE

DREAMING FOR FREUD

LOVE CHILD

ONCE WE WERE SISTERS

PENGUIN BOOKS